RESISTING HER EX'S TOUCH

BY
AMBER McKENZIE

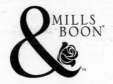

MILLS & BOON

Published in Great Britain 2014
by Mills & Boon, an imprint of Harlequin (UK) Limited,
Eton House, 18-24 Paradise Road, Richmond, Surrey, TW9 1SR

© 2014 Amber Whitford-McKenzie

ISBN: 978 0 263 90748 3

Anger became the dominant emotion as she turned to look at Matt. He was asleep on top of the blankets with one arm extended across her.

That explained the weight.

He was wearing a ragged Brown University T-shirt and jeans, and looked too much like the old Matt—her Matt.

As if on cue he opened his eyes, and a few inches away she saw the familiar blue that looked softer than she had seen it since their reunion. Her heart fluttered and she forgot her anger. He didn't say anything, and she was too overwhelmed with memories of the past to tear her eyes from his, still trying to understand the man she'd thought she once knew.

His eyes didn't have the answers—seemed only to have more questions for her. She watched as he propped himself up on one arm. His other hand moved from her waist to the side of her face, his wide palm spanning her cheek, his fingertip... eyes chan... ned and...

Dear Reader

It is my true belief that at the heart of every woman is a romantic. In some way or another we all envisage our hero and the moments that will perhaps change our lives forever. My parents, however, raised a very practical young woman who was taught from an early age not to look for a hero to complete me, but instead to complement and enrich a life I had built for myself.

Throughout my prolonged fourteen years in postsecondary education I gained that partner, and a further respect for my parents' teaching. I have been privileged to have met and worked with some of the finest, most beautiful and most dedicated female physicians around. By the end of my training, when life was moving away from textbooks and on to ways to maintain a decent work/life balance, a spark began to burn.

As a lifelong reader of Harlequin Mills & Boon® books, I always had dreams of what I considered the perfect book—and then I realised. Who would be better heroines than my friends? Women who are gorgeous, smart and by all means successful, but maybe have some unconsidered challenges when it comes to finding love. Meet Kate, a combination of many of my friends, and aptly named, as thirty percent of my colleagues at one time were named Kate. Her story is completely original, though, featuring some of my most favorite romantic gestures, from emotional torment in the rain to forehead-kisses.

My debut novel, RESISTING HER EX'S TOUCH, is the first of hopefully many forays into the perfect romance. I hope that you fall in love and gain the same admiration that I have for the men and women who devote their lives to the world of medicine.

Amber

Amber McKenzie's love of romance and all the drama a good romance entails began in her teenage years. After a lengthy university career, multiple degrees and one formal English class, she found herself happily employed as physician and happily married to her medical school sweetheart.

She rekindled her passion for romance during her residency and began thinking of the perfect story. She quickly decided that the only thing sexier than a man in scrubs was a woman in scrubs. After finishing training and starting practice she started writing her first novel. Harlequin's *So You Think You Can Write* contest came at a perfect time, and after a few good edits from her wildlife biologist childhood best friend the manuscript was submitted and the rest is history!

Amber currently lives in Canada with her husband. She does her best to juggle her full-time medical practice with her love of writing and reading and other pursuits—from long-distance running to domestic goddess activities like cooking and quilting. Multitasking has become an art form and a way of life.

RESISTING HER EX'S TOUCH
is Amber McKenzie's debut novel
for Mills & Boon® Medical Romance™

There is nothing better in life than the people who love and support you and inspire you to be better than you ever thought you could be. My love and gratitude to my mom Linda, my ultimate best friend Jennie, and my amazing husband Kyle.

CHAPTER ONE

HER HEART POUNDED against her chest, keeping cadence with the rhythm her heeled boots made against the lino-leum floor. She had everything to lose and little to no control over an outcome that was going to decide her fu-ture. Some people would take comfort in knowing they were in the right and hadn't done anything wrong, but not Dr. Kate Spence. She had learned early in life that bad things happened whether you deserved them or not.

She walked through the corridors of Boston General with reluctant determination. For the first time in five years she felt out of place in the hospital. She was used to being in her element, dressed in surgical scrubs with her entire focus on her job as a general surgery resident. Today was different. Every fiber of her being was on alert and she was conscious of waiting for the intense foreboding sensation that had come over her in the past several weeks to be fulfilled.

After years of school and sacrifice, Kate had almost made it. She had made it as a doctor, as a surgeon, and in three months' time would be starting a fellowship in New York, in one of the most acclaimed hospitals in the country. She had three months left of residency and then she was done in Boston and on her way to New

York to complete her final training and have a second chance at a new beginning.

They had called it a strategy meeting, whatever that was supposed to mean. The only thing that had registered with Kate was that they were going to have to talk about "that night" and the guilt was overwhelming.

Kate took a deep breath and tried to gather her mind and her facial expression into that of the composed professional she was widely regarded as being. She was the chief resident of general surgery in one of the nation's top five surgical programs. She arrived at work no later than five-thirty every morning and was never home before seven—and that was on evenings when she got home, because most nights she stayed and operated. Being in the operating room, fixing people, had become her salvation in life. She loved the feeling of working meticulously at something, never knowing what challenges lay inside and pushing herself to overcome all the difficulties and limitations that could arise.

In a place where things could easily get out of control, Kate felt the most in control, confident in her ability to get the job done and do what was needed for her patient.

Kate pushed through the frosted glass door leading to the conference room and took in the scene. Sitting at the large wooden conference table were all of the expected people. The hospital's chief executive officer, lawyer, chief of staff, and Dr. Tate Reed, Vascular Surgeon, her co-defendant and ex-boyfriend as of six months ago.

She knew this wasn't going to be easy, but it still hurt more than she had prepared herself for. No one liked facing their own mistakes and Kate rarely made mistakes. She had taken an oath to do no harm and had promised herself years ago that she would never be responsible for causing someone she loved pain, and she hadn't until Tate. It had been six months and every day she regretted what had happened between them. She had never fallen in love with him and that horrible night she had been forced to accept that he wasn't the man for her no matter how hard she had tried to feel otherwise.

When she walked in, every face peered up at her with acknowledgement, except for one, who refused to acknowledge her presence.

"Good afternoon Dr. Spence, please take a seat," Dr. Williamson, the chief of staff instructed.

Then and only then did he look up and their eyes meet. The same combination of hurt and anger that had been there six months earlier stared back at her. The worst part was that she knew she deserved it. She felt every muscle in her face strain as she struggled to maintain a neutral expression and conceal the feelings of hurt and regret she felt every time she thought of Tate.

Kate walked towards one of the two empty places at the conference table, choosing the one farthest from Tate. She sat down in the leather chair and wished she could just keep sinking. She looked away and focused her gaze towards the other men, reminding herself that she needed to stay confident and collected. She was the only woman in a room full of the hospital's most prominent male leaders. There would be plenty of time for guilt and remorse to torture her thoughts later, without an audience.

Jeff Sutherland, the hospital's lawyer, started the meeting. "As you all know, four weeks ago Boston General, Dr. Reed, Dr. Spence and several other hospital personnel were served with a multimillion-dollar lawsuit for wrongful death on behalf of the Weber family. The lawsuit alleges that there was a critical delay in Mr.

Weber reaching the operating room, which lead to his death, and that had he received more timely medical and surgical attention he could have survived his condition."

"They're wrong," Tate responded unequivocally.

Jeff looked up briefly, but continued. "In their affidavit, the Weber family alleges there was a twenty-minute delay and critical time lost between the diagnosis of Michael Weber's ruptured aortic aneurysm and Dr. Spence's ability to locate Dr. Reed and communicate the findings. Mr. Weber subsequently did not reach the operating room until fifty-five minutes following diagnosis, and by that time was so unstable that he did not survive attempts made by Dr. Reed to repair the aneurysm."

"He was never going to survive," Kate said. She replayed the images of the night in her mind, as she had a countless number of times. That night the happiness then the devastation, the genuine love, followed by pain and loss, had been heartbreaking. It had been the first and only time she had ever wanted out of a case, not to be in the operating room. Working across the table from Tate, knowing it was hopeless, knowing there was nothing left for Mr. Weber or for them. For the first time in her career she had felt like a coward because she hadn't been able to bring herself to confront Tate with the futility of their actions. She didn't know if it had been because of what had happened between them or if it had been because on that night she had been unable to bear the prospect of telling Mrs. Weber the man she loved was gone.

Dr. Williamson spoke. "Tate, I have reviewed this case, and in my medical opinion and in the opinion of this hospital you acted in an appropriate and timely manner in your complete care of Mr. Weber. His condition was such that even with immediate surgical intervention he was unlikely to have survived such an extensive rupture. Most vascular surgeons would not have even attempted surgical management, and unfortunately because you did you are now the target of the family's grief."

Kate exhaled for what felt like the first time since she had entered the room, grateful for a small reprieve from the nightmare.

"Thank you, David. I appreciate your support," Tate replied.

She glanced up to look at Tate, her first instinct to share their sense of relief, but he wasn't looking at her. Her relief that the chief of staff was on their side quickly left her when she remembered there was no "their" any more and that had been her choice.

She focused her attention on the chief of staff, once again mentally trying to separate her professional and personal lives. The problem was that Tate had been both. Between the demands of the hospital and the need to study whenever she wasn't at the hospital she didn't have time for a social life, but Tate had come as the complete package. They had become colleagues, then friends, and eventually lovers. Everyone had thought they were a perfect match, everyone except Kate.

Kate was forced to refocus when Dr. Williamson began speaking again.

"Unfortunately, Tate, it is more than my opinion that counts in this matter. The Weber family has been able to document and produce several witnesses who verify a twenty-minute delay in your response to Kate's repeated attempts to make contact that night. It is this evidence that has led the family to believe they have a case, and despite several medical experts, who all agree that Mr.

Weber's condition was medically and surgically futile, they are bent on having this matter argued in court."

Kate could not think of anything she wanted less and felt her stomach heave with the implications of a court hearing. The events of that night were completely entwined with every personal and private detail of her life. The thought of her personal life being discussed and examined in public, when she could barely face the details in private, was unfathomable. Kate had had six months to think about that night. Professionally, in her heart and her brain she knew that the delay had not caused Mr. Weber's death.

"In response to the legal action, the hospital has retained outside counsel to represent all parties named in the lawsuit," Jeff announced. Kate's defensive body language and Tate's unusual silence must have said more than words could express.

"Drs. Spence and Reed, this hospital expects your one hundred percent co-operation with our attorney and in all matters relating to this lawsuit," Quinn Sawyer, the chief executive officer, announced with finality. "I do not need to impress upon you the risk this hospital and your careers face if this does not go in our favor. I trust your personal relationship, whatever it may be, will not interfere with your ability to protect those interests."

"I no longer have a personal relationship with Dr. Spence."

An uncharacteristic flush burned up Kate's neck, coloring her entire face. She focused on the window, unable to face the humiliation of having her personal life referenced so openly among the most important men of the hospital. She had kept everything about her relationship with Tate private. She had never wanted anyone to think she was getting ahead by any means other than her natural surgical ability and strong work ethic, so it hurt and embarrassed her to think just how un-private things had become and what questions people would have about her now that the relationship had come to light, even if it no longer existed. She barely noticed the door open and close as she fought for control of her emotions.

"Mr. McKayne, I would like to introduce you to our senior management." Jeff's voice echoed in the background.

Kate felt her heart stop and then everything around her seemed to be suspended in time. There was no way she could have heard that correctly and she quickly turned to the door, looking for reassurance.

In as long as it took for their eyes to make contact, Kate went from pink to white. She felt a sharp pain hit her chest and tasted bile in the back of her throat. She closed her eyes, hoping for someone different to be standing at the head of the table when she reopened them. Please, not him, anyone but him, she thought, but the man standing at the front of the room was the same. He had not changed in the past ten seconds and, for the most part, not in the past nine years.

Kate was vaguely aware of introductions being shared around the table. She was falling, her mind was in free fall, overwhelmed with flashes from the past and desperately trying to reconcile what was happening in the present. Nothing that was going on inside her was in her control.

"Dr. Spence."

"Kate."

"Katherine." It was Tate's voice biting out her name for the first time in months that brought her back to the table. Tate was staring at her with a new look of confusion. She had a well-earned reputation for being focused and unshakeable, even in the worst circumstances, until today. Everyone was standing and staring at her. She rose to her feet, praying her legs would support her, and turned to face the group.

"Dr. Kate Spence, this is Matthew McKayne. He will be representing you, Dr. Reed, and the hospital in this matter."

Kate turned towards Matt and saw that his hand was outstretched towards her. The gesture was appropriate in the circumstances but completely inappropriate given their past. She didn't want to shake his hand, look at him, or want any part of him in her life. Shock evolved into anger as she once again met the eyes of the one man she never wanted to see again.

Katie was still the most beautiful girl he had ever seen, though any hint of "girl" had been replaced by a very grown-up and striking woman. Matt struggled to keep his expression neutral as he studied her. She had always been taller than most women, with both a long body and legs to match. Her figure had changed. Gone was the softness from her body and from the expression on her face. The new "Kate" that was standing before him had more of an athletic build. Her legs appeared well toned beneath her fitted dress pants and her waist was more defined, making both her hips and breasts appear more prominent and sensual. Her light blue shirt was tucked in and the top two buttons were undone, only hinting at the curves underneath.

Discomfort tore through Matt's body as he remembered the old Katie and took in the sight of new Kate. Her hair appeared darker, like a rich dark chocolate, though he couldn't tell if her hair had changed or merely now appeared darker in comparison to her pale complexion. Her skin still appeared perfect, though, with the pattern of beauty marks he could have drawn from memory.

Then he met her eyes and whatever track his mind had been on, it was sharply derailed. Katie had changed a lot in the last nine years but his enjoyment of those changes was halted by the look in her eyes. It was the same look he had seen the day he'd left, the look that had tortured him for almost a decade.

"Dr. Spence," he greeted her, the formality of calling Katie by her full title necessary but awkward on his lips. She placed her hand in his and his hand wrapped around hers as though every muscle remembered the feel of her, before she snatched it away and sat back down at the table.

Everyone else followed and Matt took the last remaining chair. That chair was next to Kate, and with his first breath he smelled the familiar scent of her rosemary and mint shampoo, which brought back more memories than the sight of her had.

His position beside her spared him from the look in her eyes. He had known he had hurt her, badly, but he had never imagined that Katie could hate him and what that would feel like face-to-face for the first time.

"Mr. McKayne, Matt, Drs. Reed and Spence have been briefed regarding the details of the lawsuit. They are aware that this hospital and its medical staff are completely behind them and their actions. They are in turn willing to work with you and your team as much as needed to resolve this matter," the CEO stated. "They have been informed that we expect an honest, full disclosure regarding all the details of that evening, so that we can resolve this lawsuit for both the hospital and the Weber family."

Matt studied the other men at the table and his focus landed on Tate Reed. In turn Tate appeared to be studying both Matt and Kate with what appeared to be hostile curiosity. He wasn't the only person who seemed to have noticed the change in her since his arrival.

"We will leave you three to co-ordinate your schedules and work on your response. Matt, if there any difficulties, in any regard, I expect to hear about them sooner rather than later," the CEO remarked to Matt, with a message that was obviously more for Kate and Tate. The group of men left and the room fell silent.

Kate and Tate remained seated at the table. Tate was looking at the pair of them intently and Kate strongly refused to look at either man. "Do you two know each other?" Tate asked.

"No," Kate responded firmly, before he could even turn to see her response to the question. When he did turn towards her, her back was straight, her head was high and she was entirely focused on Tate, dismissing Matt completely.

Tate stood from his chair and for the first time since he'd arrived, Matt took a long look at the man he was representing. Tate Reed was tall, similar in height to Matt's six feet three inches. Where Matt had dark, thick hair and the constant appearance of shadow along his jaw, Tate was dark blond and clean-shaven. Tate was well built; if paired against each other they would both probably be able to do a significant amount of damage before a victor was declared. Tate's green eyes appeared to similarly be evaluating Matt before he turned his attention back to Kate.

"I wish I could believe you, Katherine." Tate spoke, and the comment was directed only to her.

"Mr. McKayne, here is my card. I can be available to meet you when you are ready to discuss the medical facts of the case." He passed Matt the card and then shook his hand with obvious strength and power in his grip.

When the two broke apart, he turned to Kate. "Katherine, try not to make things any worse for me than you already have."

Tate left the room and Matt turned to look at Kate, who was staring intently at the door Tate had just walked through. Her gray eyes looked stricken and he felt equally struck. He recognized that look in her eyes—it was one that reflected her feelings of pain and love.

"Katie," he said softly a few moments later, his inherent need to comfort her taking precedence over the jealousy was that simmering inside him.

She flinched and turned to meet his eyes, not bothering to hide her fury. "Do not call me Katie. It's Kate or, better yet, Dr. Spence."

"Not Katherine?" He couldn't resist it, his compassion turning to jealousy and anger.

She stood from her chair and glared down at him. "I meant what I said to Tate. I don't know you and I don't want to know you. I don't know what you were thinking when you came here today, but I don't need you or your help."

"I am not sure you have a choice in that. The hospital has hired me to defend you and Dr. Reed, who, in case you haven't noticed, doesn't care what happens to you, Katie," he delivered coldly from his chair, waiting to see if he hit his mark.

He watched her response. Her gray eyes widened, initially looking hurt, then narrowed. She straightened her back and drew her shoulders down to focus on him and he felt instant unease.

"Like I said, it's Kate, and I guess that makes two of you. The difference being that I care what happens to Tate and you can go to hell." She turned and walked out of the conference room, seemingly controlled, apart from the slamming of the door behind her.

Too late, Katie, or Kate, he thought, I'm already there.

CHAPTER TWO

SHE WANTED TO run. Run to escape the confines of the hospital and her professional reputation. Run until she was so exhausted that there was no chance of being able to think about the lawsuit, Tate, or Matt. Run as far and as hard as she could until the only pain she could feel was the burning in her lungs and the tightness in her chest and not the emptiness in her heart. As she entered the hospital hallway the only other thought in her head was how to get out of the building as quickly as possible without having to talk, see, or take care of anyone else. She needed to be alone, needed to gain control of her thoughts before she risked sharing them with anyone.

"Kate!" She looked up to see her best friend, Chloe Darcy, leaning against the hallway wall, waiting for her. Chloe had been her best friend since the first day of medical school when the two women had sat next to each other, and they had been constants in each other's lives since. Chloe had chosen emergency medicine and was almost as busy as Kate. The fact that the two women still found time for each other was a tribute to the strength of their relationship. When Kate reached Chloe she felt her friend's assessment. "Do you want to talk about it?"

"No," she replied, turning her head in dissent, her eyes shut against the scene that had just unfolded.

"Okay. Is there anything I can do to make it better?" Chloe offered, not pushing Kate, as usual. Kate couldn't help but smile at her best friend. Chloe was the most beautiful person Kate had ever known, both inside and out. When they had met in medical school Kate had been an emotional disaster and most of her classmates had not made the effort to befriend her, but not Chloe. She had sat by her side daily, never prying, never pushing, just being there for the little things, until Kate had realized that she had found a true friend.

With a sense of horror Kate felt her resolve begin to crumble. Kindness at that very moment had been enough to push her over the edge. Chloe read her friend perfectly.

"Kate, let's get you out of here before you ruin your macho surgical reputation." She felt her friend's strong grip on her arm as she led her down the hall. Moments later they were in the women's change room, away from at least half of the prying eyes that filled the hospital.

"Kate, I know how private you are but sometimes it does help to talk about things." Chloe spoke quietly, her voice intentionally no louder than necessary.

Kate stared back at Chloe and knew she could tell her anything. She wanted to pour out every thought and feeling inside her in the hope that the purge would rid her of the maelstrom of emotion tormenting her. But how could you explain to someone something you couldn't bring yourself to face? "I can't, Chloe, I just can't."

It was the truth. She couldn't explain what had happened, how she was feeling, what she was going to do, what she should do, and she couldn't talk about Matt and Tate without completely breaking what little of herself she felt she was still holding together.

Chloe stepped back and Kate could tell she wanted say something and was choosing her words carefully. "Kate, you are one of the strongest women I know and there is nothing you cannot do or overcome. You just need to remind yourself of that more often."

Perfection, thought Kate. Chloe was always perfect in her words and in her support and her friendship. At that moment Chloe felt like the only secure thing in her life and more than she deserved. "Thank you. You're not so bad yourself." She smiled weakly at the understatement.

"Keep that in mind, Kate. You can't keep living your life holding everything on the inside and hidden from those who love and care about you." It was the closest Chloe had ever come to confronting her and she recognized the truth and sentiment behind her friend's words.

"I know." Her acknowledgement surprised even herself. It was another truth to add to the avalanche rolling through her mind and threatening to bury her. "But I can't, not here and not tonight."

"I know, Kate. I knew it wasn't going to be easy for you to see him today and I don't expect you to change overnight."

Kate blanched. How did Chloe know about Matt? She had never talked about Matt to anyone.

Chloe noted her friend's pallor and lowered her voice even further to ensure complete privacy. "Kate, are you sure you are okay with Tate and I still being friends? You need to be honest with me and tell me if you're not."

Kate felt relief wash through her and then guilt for focusing on Matt and forgetting the significance of today's meeting with Tate. Chloe had been talking about

Tate. There was no one other than she and Matt who knew about their past together. Matt was her past and even though he was forcing himself back into her present, what had happened between them was something she had never told anyone about, and she only hoped he had done the same.

Chloe was staring, waiting for a response, and she had to think hard to remember the question.

"Chloe, you are an amazing friend to me and to anyone else you decide to be friends with. If feeling worse about what happened with Tate was possible, thinking that I ruined your friendship with him would make it so."

She reached over and hugged her friend, trying to convey her emotions with the uncharacteristic action.

"I need to get out of here. Thank you, Chloe, for being my friend and knowing me better than I know myself sometimes."

"Always." Chloe smiled.

It was raining and she didn't care. She didn't even attempt to avoid puddles as she ran along the trail parallel to the Charles River. She let her feet strike the wet pavement as music blared in her ears and she tried to free herself from the memories that had been flooding her mind since the initial shock of seeing Matt again had worn off. The cold spring rain hit her face and blended with the warm tears that streamed from her eyes. Classic Kate, she chastised herself. Hold everything in as though nothing is wrong and then cry alone so no one can see that you are hurting, so no one thinks you are weak. The irony was that it made her feel even weaker.

As the miles passed she forced herself to accept that Matt McKayne was back in her life and she had no idea why or what he wanted. All she knew was that it was going to be hard, maybe impossible to be around Matt again. For their entire relationship she would have sworn that she knew Matt better than anyone else in the world. Then he had completely proved her wrong and now he was a familiar stranger. A stranger whose motivations and actions she couldn't predict and didn't understand. That alone terrified her, but not as much as the feelings she experienced, seeing and being near him again.

She could still describe every inch of Matt—except after today she couldn't tell if her mind had downplayed his features or if he had become even more beautiful in the intervening years. She hated it that she'd noticed, even in that brief time she had seen him. Hated it that when he'd sat next to her she had recognized his scent. But what she really hated was that when Matt had been sitting next to her, her body had remembered him in all the wrong ways. While the sharp pain in her chest had resurfaced, so had the flood of heat and spasms of attraction that had rippled through her body, the latter being responsible for her shortness of breath.

Even now in the cold rain she could still remember what is was like to be with Matt, and the combination of desire and pain associated with the memory kept her running.

She was being punished, that was the only conclusion she could settle on. This was karma because she had done to Tate what Matt had done to her, and now she was being served up the consequences. She could remember every second of their breakup, recognizing Tate's look of disbelief and hurt as the one she had worn after Matt had walked out on her. It felt hypocritical to feel this much anger towards Matt, knowing that she wasn't any better than he was, but it didn't matter. It didn't stop her from feeling like there was not enough air and that what was left of her heart was going to die. It didn't stop the desire to rip into his chest to confirm the heart she'd thought had loved her was not actually there.

She pushed forward, harder, resolving to herself that even though she had hurt Tate, at least the reason she had broken up with him was because it had been the right thing to do for Tate. Matt had broken her heart because it had been the right thing for Matt.

It was dark when Kate started to make her way home. Her apartment was a one-bedroom in a brownstone that had been divided up for rental. It was small and cheap, but it was one of her favorite places in the world. It was the place where no one put demands on her and she could let herself be who she needed to be and not what people expected of her.

Kate had spent a lot of time making her apartment the home she craved and needed. She had chosen the soft cream paint that adorned the walls. Over time she had saved and slowly put together the furniture that made her house a home. The antique wood that filled the space was precious both because of the money it had taken to purchase it and because of the time, her limited time, it had taken to find it at markets and small town shops nearby. Her favorite spot was the deep, wide, soft yellow couch that she probably slept on more than her bed. It was where she felt at peace and that thought propelled her forward to home as her body screamed at her to stop running.

The cold had finally started to set in as she rounded the final corner to her apartment. She knew her clothes were soaked through and she felt the squish of her feet in the watery soles of her shoes. All she could think of was a hot shower and curling up on her couch with her favorite charcoal throw, away from all the memories that were tormenting her.

She didn't see him in the darkness until she started up the brownstone's stairs. Her first reaction was fear at the sight of the large man tucked under the staircase awning out of the rain; her second thought was still one of fear when she recognized that man as Matt.

Stay away, her mind screamed at her. She refused to acknowledge him as she reached the door and tried to free her key from inside the wristband she wore for running.

"Katie." He said her name, asking her with his tone to acknowledge him.

"I can't talk to you right now. You need to leave," she said, not looking at him and trying to focus on the task at hand.

"I'm not leaving, Kate," he replied with a firmness that left her little doubt of her inability to dismiss him.

"Yes, you can, and you did," she said flatly, staring ahead at the door and refusing to give him any more notice. She didn't trust herself to look at him so instead looked away. Her attention was drawn to her hands, which were shaking. Her whole body was shaking and the key, which she had managed to get out, dropped onto the concrete step.

"I'm cold," she declared, hoping he would believe that was the reason for the tremors that were starting to overtake her body.

He didn't reply. Before she had a chance, he bent down and picked up the key and used it to unlock the building's front door. He walked through and held the door open, waiting for her to follow. She didn't. She stood under the awning, staring at him with a sense of panic that was building at the thought of him in her home.

"Kate, you are wet and probably freezing. Please, just come inside. I promise you can despise me just as much from in there." His new position in front of her forced her to look at him for the first time and she was immediately drawn to his face and eyes. She recognized his expression of concern and it brought her back to all the other times she had thought Matt cared for her. Familiarity propelled her forward.

Once she was inside the building, the warm air and bright lighting brought Kate back to the present. Matt was tall and overpowering in the small entryway. His hair was damp and had started to curl slightly at the ends. The angle of his jaw and the rigid way he held his shoulders gave Kate some indication that he shared her tension. He had changed out of his business suit but was no less stunning in an open leather jacket and dark blue striped shirt that he had left untucked from the jeans, which hugged low on his hips. His sexual power was breathtaking, and she struggled to get her breath back and gain control of the situation.

Never before had she felt self-conscious about her running clothes. But at this moment she desperately wished to be wearing anything other than the black tights and fitted heather-blue base layer top that provided her protection from the cold, but no modesty, outlining every curve of her body. She crossed her arms across her chest and held out one palm.

"Keys?" she asked, trying to adopt the same tone she used in the operating room when calling for an instrument.

He didn't yield and her sense of discomfort was replaced by anger. "Not until I'm sure you are okay."

When had it started to matter whether she was okay or not? It hadn't mattered to Matt nine years ago, and even though she felt far from okay, she resented his concern.

"I'm not your responsibility, Matt. You don't get to worry about me," she ground out. She tilted her head upwards, trying to make up the six-inch difference in their height, and held his gaze.

"Easier said than done," he sighed, and started climbing the stairs towards the second floor. His long legs took the stairs two at a time and before she could react he was at the top.

Not in her home, she thought. Matt could not go into her apartment, her home. It was her refuge, her place where no memories of Matt existed.

She reacted quickly to this thought, running up the stairs and without thinking, wedged herself between him and the apartment door. He wasn't ready for her movement and his body followed through on its planned course, causing him to fall against her.

She was pressed between Matt and the door, and she didn't know which one felt harder against her. She started to shake and felt warmth spread through her, his warmth. She could feel every contour of his chest through his open jacket, his shirt slowly dampening from her wet body. He instinctively widened his stance and braced himself with a hand on the door behind her to keep himself from falling any further forward into her. She ended up nestled between his legs, pelvis to pelvis, his upper body bracing over her.

Instinctively, she pressed into him and felt the hard ridge that was increasing in prominence. Beyond the slow roar that was filling her head she heard a small gasp but couldn't tell if it came from him or her. She wasn't sure how long they stood pressed against each other, until she felt him pull away at the same time he brought his forehead down to rest against hers, his eyes closed.

"Why?" he demanded quietly.

"Why what?" she whispered, confused and trying to block out the sense of loss his body's retreat had caused.

"Why don't you want me in your apartment? Is it about him? Is Tate Reed in there, waiting for you?" His voice was accusing, each new question seeming more condemning than the next. But he kept asking, not pausing, as though not wanting to hear her actual response.

Tate. Every warm enticing feeling she was having left her and she felt cold again as guilt washed over her. She tried to move even further back but felt the wood of the door against her. Tate loved her, Matt had never loved her, and she felt empty inside, thinking about both men.

"I'm not discussing my relationship with Tate with you and you have no right to ask me," she whispered, not being able to bring her voice above the intimacy his question had possessed but still containing the outrage she felt. "You need to leave."

He didn't reply. He simply lifted his forehead, replacing it with his lips. She felt both heat and memories surge through her before he backed away and pressed her key into her hand. She remained against the door as she watched him leave, not trusting herself to move until he was gone.

She wasn't sure how long she stood against the door even after he left. She felt like part of the wood, except for the small spot where her forehead burned with the memory of his soft lips pressed against her. It took hearing the beat of her shivering against the door to force her into action. She walked through the apartment in the dark, removing her clothes and leaving them in a wet trail behind her.

She stepped into the shower consumed by the cold inside and out. She had loved Matt then she had hated him, and now she had no idea how to feel. Part of her wanted to act out for the first time in her life and force him to tell her why. Why had he done it? But her instinct for self-preservation was stronger. No matter what she had told herself about why Matt had left, it would hurt more to hear him say it aloud. Seeing him today had not only brought out her anger but also unleashed every painful question and feeling of self-doubt she had tried to bury away and forget.

It took the water transitioning to cold before she thought of leaving the shower. She changed into scrub bottoms and a cotton tank top and ate the only thing she had the energy to prepare for supper— toast. It wasn't long before she was lying on the soft yellow couch cocooned within the gray blanket, trying to focus on her medical textbook and not the memories that kept replaying in her mind.

As a child she had been outgoing and bright, ready to tackle and succeed at every challenge presented to her. She had been fearless with the knowledge that her parents had always been behind her, supporting her and loving her. Then things had changed when she was eleven. Her mother had been diagnosed with breast cancer and for two years everything had focused on her mother and the disease. Kate had watched helplessly as nothing had worked, nothing had made things better, for her mother or her family.

She'd died when Kate was thirteen and from then on her family had no longer existed. She remembered one of their last moments together at the hospice. Her father had been sobbing and with what little energy she'd had her mother had stroked her hair and told her not to cry. And she hadn't.

Without her, Kate had felt lost, but not as lost as her father had. Kate's parents had been the loves of each other's lives, and without her mother Kate's dad had withdrawn from life and from his daughter. She had lost both parents, one to cancer and the other to depression, which as a thirteen-year-old she'd had no capacity to understand.

Kate's memories of middle and high school were not normal ones, something she had realized but didn't have time to care about. She spent those years trying to be the perfect daughter, student, homemaker, and friend to her dad, anything to make him happy, to make him come back to her. She hid every feeling of unhappiness and loneliness away, afraid that her pain would make her father worse and ruin what little they had together. She never discussed her mother and carried her grief alone. Every new womanly feeling or change she experienced she ignored, because it hurt too much to miss the mother she wanted to share those moments with.

Kate was terrified to graduate from high school, knowing that it meant she would have to leave home and her dad. It wasn't until she arrived at Brown University and had some time on her own that she realized how different she was from the other students, especially the other girls. They all seemed so beautiful and confident and, next to them, she felt completely inadequate and unprepared for life as a woman. She went home every weekend, not just to see her dad but also to escape the weekend social gatherings where she felt so out of place.

This eventually became a comfortable routine that lasted three years, until one weekend she came home and her dad introduced her to Julia. Her father had found love again and for the first time since her mother's death he was happy. Kate shared his happiness and at the same time felt her feelings of loneliness hit rock bottom.

Watching her father and Julia made her feel even more alone than she had before because they were together, a team, and she had no one. It was no longer necessary for her dad to be her focus in life, and she was now being forced to focus on herself and she didn't even know who she was or who she wanted to be. All her anxieties and feelings of inadequacy battered her every solitary moment while she continued to play the role of the perfect daughter, stepdaughter and student. Her dedication towards a career in medicine was her only life raft in the storm in which she found herself.

She met Matt three months later and her world changed. She had been studying at her favorite coffeehouse when she glanced up and saw the most attractive man she had ever seen in her life. The glance had easily turned into an irresistible stare. He was tall and broad shouldered with thick dark hair and piercing blue eyes. He was standing beside her table and it took her an embarrassing amount of time to acknowledge to herself that he was talking to her and to figure out what he had said. He asked to share her table, because it had an electrical outlet in the wall beside it for his laptop computer.

Previously, she would have just offered him the table, making some excuse as to why she needed to leave, but she was so drawn in by everything about him that she just managed to say yes and slide her own computer toward her to make space. He thanked her and while he started studying, her mind completely shifted, thinking only of him. He was perfection. His strong jaw was covered with a shadow of stubble that screamed masculinity to her. A gray T-shirt spanned his broad chest so that she could see the outline of every muscle group she had just been studying attentively in her textbook before he'd joined her. His shoulders led to muscular tanned arms and hands that were twice the size of hers. She could imagine the strength in his hands and what it would feel like to be held by him, to feel his jaw brush against hers, to press against his strong frame.

She started and blushed when his voice broke through her thoughts with an offer to buy her coffee. She barely managed to tell him her order without stammering, feeling completely stunned by the most outrageous thoughts she had ever had and insecure with her inexperience.

When he returned to the table with their drinks he didn't reopen his computer. He introduced himself and she was drawn in by the kindness and genuine interest she saw in his eyes. There was something about Matt that had made her feel instantly safe, and with that feeling grew the confidence she had been lacking. They spent the rest of the afternoon talking and Kate felt more important in those few hours than she had in years.

In the course of their conversation she learned about his long-distance girlfriend and on hearing that felt crushed and disappointed, but still intrigued by the man who already had someone special in his life and was still interested in her, even if she wasn't girlfriend material. The more they talked the more she liked him and the more she wanted him in her life, no matter what he had to offer.

And that was exactly what followed. At first they would see each other casually, both studying. Matt was pre-law and she was pre-med, which meant they studied a lot. She got used to him joining her on Saturday and Sunday afternoons at the coffee shop, and even had the confidence to join his table when he arrived there first. The only time she didn't see him was when he went back to New York for a weekend with his family and girlfriend, though he never talked about the visits and she didn't ask. They eventually started meeting outside of the coffee shop and beyond studying, until they were together several times a week and spoke on the phone daily.

It was hard for her to understand her feelings. Matt was her first university friend, her first male friend, and eventually her best friend. She didn't know how to sort out what she felt for him as her friend from what she assumed were normal feelings of attraction any woman would have in Matt's presence. Part of her was actually relieved to be having the same thoughts and feelings about a man that she had heard other women talking about; it made her feel normal.

One Saturday she didn't show up at the coffee shop, like she normally did. Even though they didn't have formal plans to meet, Matt came to her apartment early that afternoon to check on her and see why she had been absent from the routine they had perfected over months. She hadn't expected that. If she had she wouldn't have answered the door. Instead she answered the door in jogging pants and an oversized sweater, her face red and swollen from hours of crying. He didn't let her turn him away and on the eighth anniversary of her mother's death Kate allowed her emotions to show and cried in front of someone else for the first time since her mother had died.

She couldn't have asked for more in Matt's response. He held her until her tears subsided and then listened as she talked about her parents and what she had lost. For the first time her feelings didn't make her feel weak and helpless. Matt made her feel he understood in his responses and desire to listen. They talked for hours and he discussed his own father's death, which helped her feel normal and less like the poor orphan she had perceived herself to be. When she was finally spent of emotions and words, she fell asleep on her couch, Matt still sitting at the end. She could remember the strength of his arms around her as he picked her up and carried her to her bed, the tenderness and caring as he laid her down and covered her, and the weight of his lips against her forehead as he kissed her good-night. And her last thought as she drifted to sleep was that she was in love with her best friend.

Kate woke to the darkness of the living room lit only by the soft glow of the end table lamp. She struggled to adjust her eyes to the lighting and the reality of her surroundings. She wasn't in her old college apartment and the dreams she'd had of her past had been just that, dreams, followed by a harsh reality. She glanced over at the clock on the microwave—four o'clock in the morning. No hope of getting back to sleep, she thought.

She stretched; her neck had a kink in it from falling asleep on the arm of the couch and her legs ached from pushing too hard on her run, but she was also acutely aware of the deep ache and warmth in her pelvis. She could still feel the memory of Matt's lips against her forehead, his body pressed against hers, and the feel of him wanting her, both past and present. It made no sense. She cringed, thinking about the last time she had felt that need from him and the disaster and complete and utter devastation she had felt afterwards.

Anger overtook her as her feet hit the cold wooden floor and she walked towards her bedroom. She didn't want to remember every detail of their relationship and that night. She didn't want to still feel what it was like to be touched by him. She didn't want to still feel the pain of rejection and betrayal. She didn't want to feel anything for Matt McKayne.

CHAPTER THREE

THIRTY HOURS INTO her shift Kate's pager blared through her dictation as she described the detailed steps she had taken to resect the necrotic bowel and anastomose the viable segments. She paused in mid-sentence, her usual rhythm interrupted by the reminder tone that followed. She pressed the pager's recall button and the hospital switchboard extension flashed back at her.

Dread filled her. She was between surgical cases and had two consultations in the emergency department to review. One more interruption and there would be no chance of getting to the washroom between cases. She had long ago given up the hope of eating any time soon and sleep was like a mirage in the desert to her.

She signed off the dictation and dialed the digits she knew by heart.

"It's Dr. Spence from General Surgery. I have an outside call."

"Yes, Dr. Spence, I'll put him through."

"Kate, it's Matt, we need to talk." She had been correct with her feeling of dread. Years ago those words would have changed her world, but now they left her with a sense of foreboding.

"Why are you calling me?" The question didn't make sense as he had already stated his intentions, but it was the first thought that came to mind. Why? Why was he back?

He sighed and she sensed his impatience. Tough, she thought. "Kate, we need to discuss the details of the case, the sooner the better."

The case, of course he wanted to talk about the case. How could she have forgotten the lawsuit? It was threatening to destroy her career and now was wreaking havoc on her personal life as well. She had received notification from the New York Medical Board that her medical license for the state was on hold and would not be granted until the lawsuit was resolved. No license meant no hospital privileges, which meant no fellowship for Kate. Everything she had worked for was now in Matt's hands. Even with that in mind, she wasn't ready to face Matt again. She couldn't guarantee he would stick to the script of the present, and the past was too much to add to her fragile state of mind.

"I don't have any spare time, Matt." It was true.

"Make time, Kate, or I'll make it for you." It didn't sound like a threat, more like a fact, and something she knew he was capable of following through on. If they lost the lawsuit she was going to find it next to impossible to find employment anywhere else and she couldn't afford to burn her bridges with the hospital administration who had already warned her they expected her full co-operation.

"I'm not working this weekend." She dragged the words from herself like a confession.

"Let's meet Saturday afternoon. Do you have a preferred café you go to?"

No, she thought. There was no place she would prefer to meet with Matt. She needed to keep focused on what his new role was in her life, and the lawsuit. "We can use one of the hospital boardrooms." She had perfected her professional veneer within the hospital and if she had any hope of maintaining it with Matt, it would be here at the hospital.

"I'll see you Saturday at two. Goodbye, Kate." Such a simple word, but it wasn't goodbye.

Matt strode through the halls of Boston General on his way to meet Dr. Reed. Half of his attention was spent looking for Katie, Kate, the other half trying to decide whether he could truly represent Tate Reed. As a lawyer his job was to act in the best interests of his clients, but how could he do that for the man who had the one thing in life he wanted—Kate. One thing he did know, legally, if not personally, was that Tate and Kate were in this as a pair, and if he wanted to represent her then he had to agree to defend Tate Reed as well. And he needed to defend Kate.

Matt found the department of general surgery and made his way towards Tate's office. Along the wall of the main corridor hung the yearly photographs of everyone who had been in the residency training program. Matt stopped and examined the last five years. Kate was in all the photos, each year changing just slightly, but enough that between the first and last photos she appeared to have become not only more beautiful but more confident and mature.

He moved to the closed door with Dr. Reed's name on it and knocked louder than he'd intended. It also took longer than he expected before Dr. Reed opened the door. As he stepped into the office he was surprised to see a beautiful red-headed woman standing in the center of the room.

"Matt McKayne, this is Chloe Darcy. Chloe is in

Emergency Medicine here at Boston General," Tate said by way of introduction. "Chloe, Matt is a lawyer specializing in medical defense and has been hired by the hospital to represent Katherine and I in the lawsuit."

Chloe looked at him appraisingly. "Nice to meet you." She reached out and shook his hand. "Are you any good?"

Matt was surprised by the question and instantly liked her. "I'm very good, Dr. Darcy."

"Call me Chloe, and I am very happy to hear that. The last thing Kate needs is for this to drag on."

"You know Dr. Spence?" he asked, trying to sound professional while struggling to understand the network of relationships going on around him.

She smiled. "I know Kate probably better than anyone. I've been her best friend for the past nine years."

So Chloe Darcy was Kate's best friend and she knew her better than anyone, but apparently knew nothing about him. He assumed that because she showed no signs of hostility towards him. Tate, who, it seemed, had replaced him in Kate's life, also didn't seem to have any knowledge about their past together.

"Chloe, Matt and I have an appointment. I'll talk to you later."

"Don't worry about it. I'm not going anywhere," Chloe stated flatly. Both men watched as she left the room, closing the door a little too forcefully for it to have been accidental.

"Have a seat." Tate gestured to one of the two chairs opposite his large wooden desk and returned to his position behind the desk. He was taking charge and Matt let him. The more in control Tate felt the less likely he was to be defensive and hold things back from him. He had a lot of questions and not all of them were professional.

"I won't waste your time or mine, Dr. Reed," Matt opened, looking at him directly.

"I appreciate that. Call me Tate." He returned the challenge in his gaze, and Matt grudgingly respected the man for not backing down.

"I have thoroughly reviewed the file, as have our medical experts. The unanimous opinion is that Mr. Weber's condition was not survivable. He would not have survived even with immediate medical attention. My concern is that if this case goes to a jury they will not appropriately focus on that fact." Matt waited for his reaction.

"What is it exactly you think will be distracting them?" Tate questioned, examining Matt as intently as he was being examined. Tate was trying to gauge what Matt did and did not know, and in that moment Matt knew he was right about the nature of the relationship between Tate and Kate.

"Your relationship with Kate Spence," he responded and then in silence waited for the other man to give him the details he unwillingly craved.

"I don't have a relationship with Katherine Spence," Tate stated coldly.

Matt recognized the defensiveness in Tate's tone and decided to change tactics before Tate completely shut down. "Why do you refer to her as Katherine when everyone seems to call her Kate?"

"Old habit, I guess. The rhyming of Kate and Tate is too nauseating. Either way, it won't be an issue for much longer."

"Why not?" Matt asked, still searching for answers and what Tate was not saying.

"Katherine, or Kate, will be moving to New York in

the summer to start her fellowship in breast oncology and reconstruction."

Matt processed the information. He remembered the afternoon he'd found her crying in her apartment. He had never before felt so helpless. It hadn't been that he had never seen a woman cry—his mother and sister were known for their histrionics—but Kate had been crying from a genuine feeling of pain and not as a means of manipulation. Her career choice made perfect sense and he wondered if it was the one thing she needed to be able to finally make peace with her mother's death. If it was, he wasn't going to let anything stand in her way.

"Is there anything else you would like to tell me about you and Kate?" Matt asked directly, determined to find out the details of their relationship.

"No," Tate snapped. This time Matt was sure there was something to tell.

"Tate, I'm going to be honest with you. With expert medical opinion on our side, the hospital has no intention of settling this lawsuit. Which means that the Webers' attorneys are going to start digging, if they haven't already. They are going to talk your friends, nurses, residents, your colleagues, anyone, in the hope of finding something seemingly improper in your and Kate's actions that night. So if your goal is to protect your privacy, the best way to do that is to tell me exactly what your relationship with Kate Spence is and what happened that night. If you tell me the truth, I can find a way keep this out of court." Matt seemed to have gotten somewhere with his direct attack, because Tate grimaced and leaned forward in his chair, his arms on his desk. Matt recognized the haunted look in his eyes.

"Katherine and I had been involved in a personal relationship. It ended six months ago," Tate stated flatly. Surprising how a statement, which revealed next to nothing and contained what he already knew, still felt like a sucker punch. Once again his feelings towards Tate shifted. Any burgeoning thoughts of liking the man came to an abrupt end and he felt a masochistic need to know more.

"You are going to need to do better than that," Matt replied, unable to keep his tone neutral.

"Fine. Katherine and I had been seeing each for a year and a half," Tate answered, still barely budging on what Matt needed to know, more personally than professionally.

"Was it serious?" That was as close as he could get to asking if they had been lovers.

"For one of us." Matt didn't want to hear any more. He had made some very hard decisions years ago with regard to Kate. Decisions he had justified as being the best for her. Now to hear that instead of living the perfect life he had hoped for her, Kate had fallen in love with a man who hadn't loved her back was a bitter pill to swallow. More so when he thought of the way she had reacted when the two men had been introduced; she still loved Tate even though he didn't love her.

Matt studied the man sitting across from him, but then realized, to be honest; he had let Kate go too. So he wasn't any better, despite his intentions. He then straightened in his chair and began a new resolve to remain professional and get through this meeting before he said or did something he would regret.

"Six months ago. So the time your relationship ended was the same time of Mr. Weber's death? If the two events are linked, I need to know." Matt noticed Tate's attitude change from adversarial to sad; maybe the man realized what he had given up. Tate's shoulders had fallen and he no longer looked at Matt. Time passed and Matt thought Tate wasn't going to answer. Then he heard a deep breath and a less assured voice started.

"Kate and I broke up the same night Mr. Weber died. We saw each other earlier in the evening and later that same night she was called into the hospital to cover for one of the other senior surgery residents who had to leave with the transplant team. I was on second call for Vascular Surgery."

"What was her state of mind?" Matt asked, his worry for Kate, even past Kate, taking precedence.

"I think you should ask her that," Tate answered.

"I'm asking you. I need to know the impression she gave that night."

"She had been surprised. She said she hadn't seen it coming." He was nodding, as if remembering the evening and confirming to himself how it had been.

"Then?" More and more this felt like watching a car accident in slow motion when you knew it was not going to end well but you couldn't look away.

"She was the most upset I had ever seen her and she left." Was that regret he heard in Tate's voice? But before he could examine the thought further, Tate was continuing. "However, when I saw Katherine later in the operating room and throughout all of our medical interactions that night she was one hundred percent professional and composed."

So Tate was going to back and defend Kate. That was going to make the case easier to defend, but Matt wondered about what was motivating the gesture. Was it professionalism, honesty, guilt from breaking off their relationship or part of a plan to win her back?

"Can you explain the time lag between her first attempt to contact you and the response?" Matt asked. Gone was any desire he had to continue this conversation. He actually wanted to leave and get away from the memories of Kate that were filling his mind. Kate with that look of shock and pain filling her eyes. Had she looked the same for Tate?

"Katherine had been surprised. I honestly don't think she had expected anything that happened that night. After she left my loft and things started to sink in, she wanted to talk. She called and I told her there was nothing more to discuss. She called a few more times shortly after that and I ignored her calls. A few hours later when she called on my cellphone to discuss Mr. Weber, I didn't realize her focus had shifted and I again ignored her attempts to talk to me. It wasn't until the hospital operator contacted me and patched her through that I learned about Mr. Weber."

"Does anyone else know the details of that night?"

"The only close friend Katherine confides in is Chloe Darcy."

"So Chloe is a friend of both of yours?" Matt asked, trying to understand what role Chloe Darcy had played.

"I met Chloe through Katherine. We used to spend time together as part of a social group prior to the breakup."

"And now?"

"She is Katherine's best friend. Chloe and I have never talked about that night. I'm not sure what Katherine told her, but Chloe would never do or say anything to deliberately hurt Katherine, that I'm sure of." Matt believed him. Chloe was obviously protective of Kate and he had instinctively liked and trusted her. At least Kate had one person in her life she could depend on.

"Do you think Kate has any reason to want to hurt you?" Matt pried.

"I don't understand your question, Mr. McKayne."

"Please, call me Matt. The other day Kate seemed very concerned about you and your well-being. Do you think she will vouch for your actions as clearly as you are for her?"

"Absolutely. Katherine is nothing if not honest. That night she told me she wanted desperately to be with me, to be in love with me, and I believed her. I don't think any amount of time will change that." He didn't sound arrogant and that disheartened Matt much more than the statement had.

"I would appreciate it if, when you talk to her, you could spare her the same discussion we have just had. I think the only reason this situation has developed is that the hospital gossip mill put together the timing of our break-up and Mr. Weber's death. We were both completely professional in our behavior that night and the hospital switchboard reached me within appropriate professional standards." Tate was ending their conversation and stood from his chair.

Matt conceded and stood. He paused and studied Tate's face, but the other man gave nothing away. The meeting had only generated more questions for him than answers. It had confirmed what he already knew, that Kate and Tate had been a couple. For a year and a half Tate had had Kate, and even though they had now broken up, he still had Kate. The fact that, after breaking up with her, Kate was still defending him spoke volumes about the type of man Tate was. He wanted to hate the man but couldn't, despite the jealousy that was growing inside him.

The sane part of his mind also recognized that Kate

still loved and trusted Tate, and Kate didn't do either of those things easily. She was introverted and cautious, which made her actions towards Tate even more telling. What would happen when this was done? Would they find their way back to one another? Would Tate realize what he had given up and want her back? He needed to talk to Kate and he couldn't wait one more day for his answers. The one thing Tate was definitely right about: Kate and Tate was a nauseating combo, and not just the rhyming names.

It took Kate another ten hours to complete her mental list of tasks. She had worked one of the hardest shifts in her career and she hadn't cared. She'd wanted to work, to stay busy, to avoid everything, including her own thoughts.

After going to work an hour early the previous day at five a.m., she had worked through the day, the night and well into the next evening, and it was nine o'clock on Friday night before she was ready to finally leave the building. She was exhausted, and it actually felt a relief to have that as her primary state of mind.

She yawned as she pulled off her scrubs and pulled on the same jeans and fitted long-sleeved blue shirt she had arrived in the previous day. She pulled her hair out of its ponytail and put her watch on. If she hurried she could force herself to eat something and be asleep by ten. If she slept well she might actually have the focus to study tomorrow and not think about her impending meeting with Matt.

Kate walked out of the women's locker room and literally ran into Tate leaving the men's change room. She bounced off his lean frame and had to grasp the wall for support. She didn't realize whom she had hit and he looked equally surprised as she caught the moment when he recognized her. "Sorry," she said awkwardly.

He reached out to steady her, grasping her forearms and holding her until she regained her balance and straightened. "Katherine. I heard you did well last night." His tone was genuine, without the anger or hurt she had come to expect. She couldn't disguise the surprise she felt. For the first time since *that* night, the tension between them was gone. He wasn't the warm Tate she had loved, but this was better than it had been, and probably better than she deserved. She blushed, embarrassed by his kindness.

"Thank you. Your opinion means a lot to me," she replied shakily. Her exhaustion made it hard to control the feelings of relief and loss she associated with her new and old relationship with Tate.

"I spoke with our lawyer, Matt McKayne, today."

No! her mind screamed as she reached out and grasped the wall for support. She studied his face and saw no signs that he knew about her past with Matt. He would be hurt and disgusted with her if he knew. It was sickening to think about the two men together. For different reasons, she hadn't been good enough for either of them, and the thought of them discussing that fact was like a hot poker ripping through her chest. They had both been witness to her greatest inadequacies and she would rather die than have either man share their "Kate Spence" story.

"It's okay, Katherine. I told him the truth. That you are a professional, competent surgeon and that nothing in your actions that night was negligent. He knew about us, though, and was asking the details of our relationship and breakup."

She went from panic, to relief, to anger, to fear within

seconds. Matt had no right to ask about her relationship with Tate. He really had no right to ask Tate about her at all. What questions would he have for her? "What did you tell him?" She gulped.

"As much of the truth as he needed to know, while protecting both of our personal lives and reputations." She didn't need to know more. Tate would keep the personal details of their breakup to himself, for his own sake as much as hers.

"Thank you."

He stared at her, his thoughts hidden as he looked at her for an unknown answer. "Goodnight, Katherine. If it's okay by you I think I'm going to use Kate from here on in, like everyone else."

She smiled a little sadly. "I'm just happy you are planning to talk to me."

"Good night, Kate." The conversation was definitely over and Tate walked away. She wondered what had changed for him, but honestly didn't care what the impetus had been for what felt like the forgiveness she didn't deserve.

She walked through the halls of the hospital lost in her thoughts. The overhead fluorescent lights reflected off the linoleum floors as she made her way towards the glass-walled lobby. Her head felt as full as her body felt exhausted. She was grateful that she had put Matt off, even if it was only for a day. She paused at the entryway, threading her arms through the sleeves of her black wool jacket and slowly working the buttons closed to protect her from what appeared to be a cold spring night.

"Kate." In what felt like slow motion she turned towards the voice she recognized. Matt was walking towards her. He was dressed in a dark gray suit with a blue tie that matched his eyes perfectly. She felt her breath catch and a flush spread through her, her body recognizing his with appreciation. She reached up and ran her fingers through her hair, trying to tame the mess that had been tied back and stuffed under an operating-room cap all day, then stopped, catching herself in the action. It didn't matter to Matt how she looked and she no longer cared what he thought, she reminded herself.

"Matt." She forced his name out.

"We need to talk."

He looked agitated. If you didn't know him you wouldn't be able to tell, but she had known him well and recognized the subtle force in his voice and his rigid posture.

"Yes, I believe we have a meeting for tomorrow at two." She didn't have the energy to play this game. Whatever Matt had come to say to her tonight, he needed to say it and let her go home.

"I met with Tate Reed today." The statement reminded her of old legal dramas where the prosecutor baited his witness into revealing information without even asking a question.

"Yes, I know. I already talked to Tate. It appears he has already answered many of your questions about the circumstances behind the lawsuit, and other than that we have nothing to talk about." She tried to sound like her professional, confident self and force out the exhaustion and pain that made her feel unprepared to deal with Matt. He needed to know her boundaries and now was as good a time as any to make it clear what was off-limits for discussion. He didn't seem pleased with her answer.

"I don't care about Tate Reed," Matt said. Now he was definitely angry. Part of her told herself to walk away, that she wouldn't win, not against Matt and not when she was this tired. Unfortunately, the same exhaustion allowed her emotions to take over.

"You seemed to care the other night. You also seemed to care enough when you talked to Tate and asked him questions that are none of your business," she responded, matching his anger in her tone.

"Like it or not, Kate, you are my business." Mistake. She had made a critical mistake in challenging him. Now they were on a path she didn't want to be on. She didn't want to talk about them, about their past, yet couldn't hold back her reaction to his statement or the look in his eyes. He was looking at her with passion and the irony made her want to cry.

"It has never mattered what I thought or felt, has it?" She was done with being professional as she felt her personal pain seep through. She met his look and saw that she had wounded him, and it didn't make her feel any better.

"That's not true, Kate." His hands were jammed in his pockets, his shoulders pulled back, his whole stance masculine and set.

She looked at Matt and briefly remembered the girl she had been and the man she had thought he was. For the second time that night she smiled sadly then regained control of the woman she had become. "I'm not going to do this, Matt."

"Do what?" he asked, but she kept talking.

"I'm not going to talk about the past. It happened a long time ago and it doesn't matter, I've moved on with my life, without you."

"I don't believe you." And then he reached out and took her hand in his and held it hard. The touch was electric. Warmth spread through her whole body and she felt her heart start to race. She stared for a long time at his face, meshing in her mind the two versions of him. Old Matt and this Matt.

"Believe what you want, it doesn't matter to me," she sighed, pushing away the memories that statement brought forward. "Please, let go of my hand, I'm tired and I want to go home." He didn't look like he was going to let go, he just kept staring at her as if she was a puzzle he could figure out. "Please, Matt."

He released her hand. "I'm parked out front. I'll drive you home."

"No, thank you." She'd had about all the quality Matt time that she could handle and would rather walk the entire length of Boston than risk spending more time with him.

"Kate, if you don't want a scene, just get in the car and let me drive you home." It was a statement more than a threat, but coming from Matt it got her attention.

This was not the Matt she had known. She had never seen Matt lose control. He had always been calm and in control of everything, but not now. One look at his face told her to listen. His eyes were boring into her, his jaw was clenched, and she saw the small tremor that seemed to be traveling through his body. She looked around the lobby, the fluorescent lights creating an unnatural contrast to the darkness that seeped in through the glass wall from the outside. The atrium was still well populated with hospital staff, sufficient that if a scene did occur, she would be back as the number-one topic for the hospital gossips. That, combined with the look on Matt's face, that said he just might do it, and her overwhelming fatigue forced her to give in. "Okay."

She had lost the fight, and her resignation kept her from pulling away when he placed his hand on the small of her back and led her out the hospital's front entrance. His hand spanned almost the entire width of her back. Even through her coat and sweater she could still feel his warmth and the sense of protection she had always felt around Matt. She was surprised that feeling hadn't vanished from its association with him.

A car door was being opened in front of her and she got in, barely registering the car's luxury name and features. Once inside, she sank into the deep pocket of the leather seat. Matt got in the driver's side and started the engine. The air from the heating system was like warm milk to her exhaustion. He reached over and turned on her seat warmer. She didn't fight the strong urge to close her eyes, it seemed the better option to having to look at or make conversation with Matt.

She rolled over, her mind barely registering the soft pillow under her head. It wasn't until she felt the friction of the sheet against her bare abdomen and the weight spanning her body that she realized something was wrong, very wrong. She opened her eyes and found herself looking at an unfamiliar ceiling. It was a high ceiling, white, crossed with dark wooden beams. She didn't need to look to her side to know what she would find. She had always been able to sense his presence before she actually saw him.

How had she ended up here? She felt vulnerable; she was still incredibly tired, and couldn't remember how she had ended up at what she knew must be Matt's apartment. She moved again and processed that she was naked, apart from her bra and underwear. She flushed, both embarrassed and angry that Matt had taken it upon himself to undress her, that she had slept through it all, and, worst of all, that Matt had seen the dark purple lace thong and matching bra that had never been intended for anyone else's eyes.

Anger became her dominant emotion as she turned to look at Matt, who was asleep on top of the blankets with one arm extended across her. That explained the weight. He was wearing a ragged university T-shirt and jeans and looked too much like the old Matt, her Matt. As if on cue, he opened his eyes, and a few inches away she saw the familiar blue eyes that looked softer than she had seen them since their reunion. Her heart fluttered and she forgot her anger.

He didn't say anything, and she was too overwhelmed with memories of the past to tear her eyes from his, still trying to understand the man she'd once thought she knew. His eyes didn't have the answers, only more questions that he seemed to have for her. She watched as he propped himself up on one arm and his other hand moved from her waist to the side of her face, his wide palm spanning her cheek, his fingers in her hair. His eyes changed then, darkening as his pupils widened and his mouth came down on hers.

It started as a soft kiss, his lips brushing against hers. Then he pressed deeper and the pressure of his lips, the stubble brushing against her face, his hand pulling her towards him, was all-encompassing. She opened her mouth in shock and felt his tongue slip inside as he deepened the kiss. Instantly she was on fire, she could feel, smell, taste everything about him, and it inspired a passion that she hadn't felt in so long. She felt alive. She felt like herself.

Her arms reached up to wrap around him, her sudden movement causing him to move on top of her and crush her. The weight of his body on hers heightened her desire; he felt incredible and she responded to his kiss, her tongue matching his with an increasing sense of urgency. Her fingers were in his hair, pulling him closer and closer, desperately wanting to have no space, no air, nothing between them, nothing that could stop this feeling. She felt a sense of panic when she felt him lift himself from her slightly, but was rewarded when he pulled away the blankets that covered her and came back down on her.

Every part of her body yearned to be touched by him. Her breasts felt heavy and a steady throb pulsed between her thighs. She moved her hands down his wide shoulders and muscular back, feeling his hard muscles tremble in response. She grabbed his shirt in her fists and struggled to pull it over his head, until he sat up and removed the offending garment. She couldn't stand to be separated from him even for that moment, and sat up to press herself against his kneeling form. He hauled her onto his lap, her legs straddling him. She wrapped her arms around him again, feeling her breasts crush against his chest as much as they could within their constraint.

His hand swept her hair to one side as his mouth came down along the side of her neck. He licked, kissed and tasted the low part of her neck just above her collarbone and she arched her head back in response. She needed more, wanted more, wanted to ease the large ache that was growing inside her, and she moved her pelvis forward and ground into his. She was rewarded as his hard ridge pressed into her. Then she felt a new release as her bare breasts collided against his chest, her bra having been unfastened and pulled away. One hand closed over her breast, his thumb stroking the already erect and sensitized nipple.

The other hand grasped the bare bottom that her

thong exposed, trapping her against him and echoing her need to push into him. It quickly became not enough, and he pulled away and bent his head to kiss her breasts, his tongue reaching her nipples, taking time to encircle and draw each into his mouth. She pulled open his jeans, the zipper falling from the pressure of him. Her hand reached in to touch him, and she felt him contract against her.

Two hands then grasped her hips and she was moved from her straddled position. She looked up in shock but the same heat that she felt was mirrored in his eyes. She watched as he removed his jeans and boxers, leaving just him. He was fully aroused and everything about him was masculine perfection. He rejoined her on the bed and gently pushed her onto her back against the pillows. She bent her knees and spread her legs, wanting him between.

His hands tangled in her hair as he returned to kissing her, the head of his shaft now rubbing against the damp purple lace between her legs. It was the best form of torture, one where you wanted to stop because the pleasure was too intense, but at the same time knew the release would be more than worth the progression, and that was what made it unforgettable. His hand skimmed her body and ventured towards her inner thighs. She felt the lace move slightly, as his finger caressed her crease and pushed inside. She knew she was wet, and even though the penetration was not the part of him she desperately wanted inside her, she still contracted her muscles around him, both for her satisfaction and to tempt him.

It worked, and for the first time since they had awoken, words were spoken. "Oh, God, Katie, I want you so badly," he whispered against her cheek, breaking from their kiss.

His words, however softly spoken, had the opposite effect on her. Katie, she wasn't Katie any more. Katie had been the foolish girl who had fallen in love with her best friend and had had her heart broken. Katie was the girl he had walked away from and ignored. The memory of that feeling was the only emotion powerful enough to break her from the path to ultimate fulfillment that she had been on. Instantly she felt vulnerable and weak, and very exposed, which technically she was. Her hands pressed against his chest and she shoved as hard as she could.

"Stop."

He made eye contact with her, and she wasn't sure what he saw, but he moved. She scrambled off the bed and headed for the nearest door, praying it was the bathroom.

She closed what thankfully was the bathroom door and pressed her back against it. The dark, empty room calmed her growing sense of panic as she gulped for air, trying to hold back her tears. She looked around, her eyes adjusting to the city night's light filtering through the frosted window. She was in Matt's bathroom, virtually naked, only a door separating her and Matt. What had she been thinking? She hadn't. She had completely lost control; she had almost lost herself in Matt. Again. Self-loathing rose up inside her. She knew better. If anything had come from their last time together, it had been the hard truth that in life the only person she could depend on was herself, and tonight she had let herself down.

Her hand found the light switch. She blinked rapidly at the brightness and studied the reflection looking back at her in the large bathroom mirror. Her hair was wild, her lips were swollen, her cheeks showed the marks of Matt's five o'clock shadow, there was a faint mark on her left breast, and she was naked except for her purple thong. She shuddered, looking around the room for something to cover up with, needing to hide the evidence of her mistake. Her eyes fell on Matt's robe. She hated it that that was her only viable option, but nothing else in the room would provide her the coverage she desperately wanted so it would have to do. The brown terry-towel robe smelled like Matt, but she blocked that from her mind, ran the cold water and splashed it on her face.

Now what? she thought to herself. Naked Matt was on the other side of the door, waiting, probably, for an explanation. He would be waiting a long time for that, because she couldn't explain how tonight had started and had no intention of telling him why she had put an end to it.

It took another ten minutes before she was ready to leave the room, holding her breath as she opened the door. Folded up in the doorway were her clothes. Her eyes darted around the room. She saw the bed and the tangled sheets, but there was no sign of Matt. She took the clothes back into the bathroom, closed the door and dressed quickly, pulling her hair back with the extra hair tie she found in her jeans pocket. She took a final steadying breath, trying to summon the strength she was going to need to face him.

She found him in the living room, sitting on the couch, his attention fixed on the gas fireplace in the center of one of the walls. He looked up as soon as she came in. He too was fully dressed, not that it mattered as she could still see every contour of his naked body in her mind. It was a battle in her mind between the need to be with him, feel him against her, and the memories that told her to run as fast as she could and never look back. Before she could say anything he was walking towards her, reaching out with her coat and bag in his hand. He passed them over carefully so as not to touch her and gave the impression of not even wanting to be near her.

"I'll drive you home." He didn't sound like himself, but she couldn't figure out much beyond that. This was not the reaction she had expected, and while she was grateful not to have to replay the details of their encounter aloud, she was also hurt by his dismissal and couldn't control the accusation in her eyes when she looked at him again.

He misunderstood the look. "I did drive you home earlier, but when we got to your apartment I couldn't wake you up and couldn't find your keys to carry you inside. So I brought you home so you could sleep here. That's it; that's all." He sounded defensive and angry. Well, so was she.

"Thank you." The words were terse. She put on her coat and snatched her bag from his outheld hand. He grabbed his own jacket and unlocked the apartment door.

They traveled in silence down the elevator, into the parking garage and during the entire car ride back to her apartment. At three in the morning traffic was minimal, so the drive was mercifully short. Normally silence like this would be uncomfortable, but she knew talking about what had just happened between them would take discomfort to a whole new level.

Her hand was on the door handle as he pulled up in front of her building and she had the car door open before the vehicle had even come to a full stop. She needed to get away from Matt, she needed time to figure out what tonight meant, if anything. Her foot was on the curb, half-out of the car, when she heard his voice.

"He's not going to change his mind." She would have missed the words if it had not been for the dead silence of the night.

It made her pause, settling her body back into the seat. She looked back at Matt, whose hands were still gripping the steering wheel, his gaze focused straight ahead, not looking at Kate. What was he talking about? She slumped further back into the passenger seat, too thrown by his statement not to voice the thought in her head. "I don't understand."

"Tate Reed." By now he had turned to look at her, and she still didn't understand. The mention of Tate, though, brought a comparison to mind. She hadn't ever felt with Tate the way she had tonight with Matt. Never so out of control, never so desperate for release, so passionate.

"He doesn't love you," Matt stated, almost apologetically, like he was breaking bad news to a client.

It felt like a slap in the face, a reminder of another time long ago. Okay to have sex with but not worthy of love. No wonder he hadn't wanted to talk about what had almost happened between them tonight. It was no big deal for Matt, just as it hadn't been the last time. She could feel a lump start to form in the back of her throat and focused her eyes into a hard glare in effort to control the tears of humiliation that were forming at the edges.

"No, he doesn't love me any more. But he did love me and he still respects me and would never hurt me, which makes him a better man than you." She had meant to hurt him, to wound him, to have him feel some of her pain, and when she looked over and saw that she had succeeded, it didn't make her feel any better. What was she doing here with Matt? Wasn't the definition of craziness repeating the same actions again and again and expecting a different result?

"I'm a complete fool," she muttered to herself, and completed her departure by slamming the car door and not turning back to look at Matt, who remained parked outside as she entered her building. She was locked safely inside her apartment and lying in bed before she heard his car start up again and leave.

He sped through Boston's underground tunnels too angry to return to the memories that now awaited him at home. He looked at his now-empty passenger seat, remembering her in it curled up, sleeping, looking no different than she had almost a decade ago. When he had lifted her out of the car and carried her to the apartment, she had curled her arms around him and he had remembered what it had felt like when she'd been his.

When she had woken up he had seen the same trusting eyes of the past and he had been unable to resist kissing her. He didn't know what he'd meant by the kiss, he'd just felt a need to be closer to her, to regain the intimacy they had lost. The instant he had felt her lips, tasted her, he had lost all control. He shifted uncomfortably in the sports car seat, his erection returning painfully with the thought of Kate and her passionate response. The Kate he had been with tonight was not the same Katie he had known. The new Kate was no longer tentative. She had grabbed at him, moaned beneath him, had eagerly lain back and opened herself to him. Or so he had thought.

It had been a complete and sudden change, a moment of recognition. The moment she had heard his voice she had pushed him away and run. It had felt like a cold knife had stabbed him in the chest as he had felt the full impact of her rejection. He had wanted to go after her, to make her face him, but pride had held him back. He hadn't wanted or needed to hear that the reason she had stopped was because he was not the man she wanted or loved. He hadn't wanted to hear her reject him aloud, to tell him that she only wanted and loved Tate. That in her sleep-deprived state she had fantasized that he was Tate, right up until his voice had broken the illusion.

Her rejection tortured him. He never expected Kate to live a life of celibacy, but he had also deliberately chosen not to think about the alternative. Now he was faced with a reminder of the facts, what she looked like, what she felt like, how she would react and respond to the most intimate of touches, in essence how she would make love with the man she loved. And in acquiring that knowledge he was also faced with the fact that he was no longer that man.

CHAPTER FOUR

THE LOUD KNOCK brought Kate out of the darkness and forced her to open her eyes. She had been awake until six a.m., thinking about Matt, being torn between painful memories of the past and her body's frustration at its lack of fulfillment. The knock came again and Kate grabbed her bathrobe and made her way to the door.

Chloe was standing on the other side, smiling, her hair down and straightened, her casual yoga pants and V-neck shirt nicely outlining her figure. She looked perfect, and Kate shuddered at the contrast to her own disheveled appearance. Chloe must also have recognized the difference because her smile quickly vanished and her green eyes began to evaluate Kate as she would a patient. "Oh, my God, I woke you up. Are you okay? Are you sick?"

It would be so easy just to agree and send her friend away, but Kate felt like she had lied, even if by omission, more in the past few days than she had in years, and she was tired of it. That wasn't her; it wasn't who she was. "No, Chloe, I am post-call and had a late night. Come in so I can stop standing in the doorway halfnaked."

Chloe stepped through into the small kitchen and perched on a stool at the kitchen bar. Kate shut the door and joined her, starting to make coffee. "It's okay, I actually brought coffee for both of us, though by the looks of things you could use both."

Kate smiled ruefully at the comment, wondering how she could have missed the tray and bag in Chloe's hands but grateful to not have to make an effort and at the accuracy of Chloe's assessment.

"I brought the coffee and muffins in case you wanted to study together; I didn't think you would be post-call today," Chloe said.

"I'm not technically post-call. I'm post-post-call, which is normally fine except that I didn't get much sleep last night so it still feels like the day after." Kate was normally very disciplined in her post-call routine— she needed to be or the fatigue would drag on for the entire week.

"Did you have an extender shift yesterday?" Chloe asked, obviously puzzled. Kate had worked as a physician extender after her first two years of residency had ended and she had passed her basic boards. The shifts involved her being on call and available for medical emergencies in various rehabilitation facilities and nursing homes. The shifts paid well and she had needed the money to help with the massive interest payments on her student loans. Kate had had to stop taking the shifts once she had become Chief Resident because of the added workload of her new role and needing to study for her final board exams.

Kate's expression faltered at the immediate vision of Matt naked and pressed against her. She blinked, holding her eyes shut against the memory. When she opened them Chloe's face had transitioned from surprise to disbelief.

She couldn't face the look or the questions that were

about to follow, so she turned and left the kitchen, moving to the soft yellow couch, curling her legs beneath her and covering herself with the throw blanket. Chloe read her friend correctly and said nothing as she moved to follow Kate, taking a place on the opposite end of the couch. She brought her offering with her, handing Kate a muffin and pressing a coffee into her other hand. Then to Kate's surprise she didn't say anything else. She just sat, and waited.

The silence was calming. It helped Kate regain her composure and gave her time to think as opposed to react. She absently picked at the muffin, thinking through the events of the last few days, and realized that Chloe was right, she did need to learn to talk about her feelings. She needed to tell someone, needed to say the words and thoughts in her head aloud before she went crazy, rethinking, reanalyzing, reliving the same moments over and over again.

"Have you ever been in love with someone when they didn't love you back?" Kate asked, more as an explanation than a question. "When I was at university, completing my undergraduate degree, I fell in love with my best friend and in the end he didn't love me back."

"I'm sorry, Kate, but I don't understand how that connects to now."

"Tate and I broke up because he asked me to marry him. When I looked down and saw him on one knee, holding out an engagement ring, the first thought in my head was that it should have been Matt. And that was when I knew I didn't love Tate in the same way, not enough to be his wife."

"Oh." Chloe's face was beyond shocked. They had never talked about why she and Tate had ended, just that they had. She hadn't told her about the proposal or about

Matt or the role he had played. "Kate, that was months ago. What happened with Tate last night?"

"Nothing. We talked and it was nice. For the first time since we broke up I actually think he and I might be okay."

"If nothing happened with Tate, why are you tired with what appears to be stubble burn on your cheek?" Chloe asked pointedly.

Kate felt heat rise through her as her hand reached up to touch the mentioned area, feeling the change in her sensitive skin. "That's from Matt. He kissed me last night and for a few minutes I forgot about our past."

"Are we talking about the same Matt? The Matt I met yesterday? The lawyer who was meeting with Tate to discuss the case?"

"Same Matt. As luck would have it, the hospital hired my old ex to defend my new ex and me. Horrible, isn't it? The only two men I have ever been with in my entire life in a room together. I never told Tate about Matt. I didn't want to hurt him any more than I already was, and I couldn't explain how and why I still had feelings for the man who broke my heart."

"Does Matt know about your relationship with Tate?"

"Yes, but how much I don't know. He keeps making comments about Tate that I don't understand."

"Is he jealous?"

"No, of course not, he has no reason to be jealous. If he wanted me he could have had me, but he didn't. He told me to my face that he didn't love me and then walked away, back to his girlfriend, and never looked back. Jealousy implies wanting something someone else has, and Matt made it perfectly clear he didn't want me."

"If he doesn't want you, how do you explain his marks on your body?"

"I can't. Maybe he's lonely and I'm convenient, again," she sighed.

"That sounds really harsh, Kate."

"No, what's harsh is walking out on someone who maybe you didn't love but at least should have cared about enough not to obliterate her existence from your life."

"When did all that happen?"

"Right before medical school started. As you recall, I wasn't exactly coping well with life when we first met."

"Makes sense now. I wish you had told me then, though."

"Talking about it would have made it worse. As it was, it took me a long time to realize that he wasn't who I'd thought he was and we weren't what I'd thought we were."

"I'm sorry, Kate."

"Me too."

"Are you going to tell Tate about your past with Matt?" Chloe asked.

"No, it's in the past and I refuse to give Matt any more importance in my life and humiliate myself again by explaining it all to Tate."

"You're being pretty hard on yourself over this, Kate," Chloe said sympathetically.

Kate shook her head and stood from the couch. "I made a huge mistake with Matt and I refuse to risk ever repeating it."

"So if you don't have any feelings for this guy then what the hell happened last night?"

"Insanity and fatigue happened. I woke up and it was like how it used to be and for a moment it was the old Matt and the old Katie. But I guarantee you that will never happen again. I know too much about Matt. I'm not the naïve girl I once was. I have my own life now and I know that I don't need him. Even better, seeing him again has helped cure me of any lingering images I had of the guy I once loved. I know for sure that he doesn't exist and I can move on with my life."

"Kate, I hate to point out the obvious, but you do need Matt. He's your only hope for settling this lawsuit and getting your fellowship and career back on track."

"I know. I guess that is one small bright side to this situation. I know Matt and some things never change. If there's a way to win this case, he will. Matt is driven to succeed at all costs."

"That doesn't sound like the type of man you would fall for."

"It's not. The Matt I fell in love with was giving and kind. It just happens that that part of him wasn't as important to him as it was to me."

Matt walked back into the hospital the following day for his meeting with Kate, and for the first time in his career he felt completely unprepared. It was not a feeling he enjoyed. He didn't know how he would react to her, or her to him, if she would even show up after their night together.

He walked into the boardroom five minutes before their scheduled meeting and was surprised to see her already seated at the table. She was reading from a large textbook, her hands tangled up in her long brown hair. She stopped reading the moment he entered the room, her eyes rising to stare up at him.

It reminded him of their past. She had been sitting exactly the same way the first time he'd seen her. She had easily been the most beautiful woman in the café but, compared to almost all the other women he'd known, she hadn't seemed to notice or try to use it to her advantage. He had seen her in the same spot every time he'd gone to the café, until one afternoon he could no longer resist the temptation she'd presented.

Within a few hours of talking to Kate he'd known that his instincts had been dead on. She had not been like any other woman he had ever met. Matt had never been without a woman from a young age. His appearance, confidence and social status had been enough to ensure a willing and ready woman on his arm and in his bed. The fact that he'd had such a woman already in his life had not been enough to keep him from exploring Kate.

Soon she had become his favorite person, his best friend, and Matt had liked himself most when he'd been around her. He would sometimes stand back across the coffeehouse and just watch her. The intense look of concentration on her face, the way she would abstractedly run her fingers through her hair, and then she would look up and see him and smile. She had made him feel welcome and like he belonged. But that had been then, and today Kate was not smiling.

He took the seat opposite her across the table. He needed to remind himself that his purpose was the lawsuit and sitting too close to her was a distraction from that purpose.

"My firm has acquired and reviewed all the documents related to the case. There are a few depositions we need to talk about."

"Your firm?" she asked, the question holding more censure that he'd expected from her. She was still angry and he needed to do his best to calm her down if they were ever going to be able to discuss the case in a constructive manner.

"I'm a partner at my grandfather's law firm. I started and head up the medical defense division."

The McKayne family was rich and powerful and known for their prominent presence in the New York legal community. His grandfather had founded a law firm decades earlier that had grown to be one of the best, making his family very wealthy. Matt's father had been in line to succeed his grandfather until he'd died suddenly of a heart attack when Matt had been four, leaving the family's dynasty and future firmly on Matt's shoulders. Matt often wondered how different his life would have been if his father had lived.

The medical defense division was his creation and he was involved in every aspect of its operation. He represented clients but also oversaw the operations of all the firm's satellite offices, which was how he'd ended up back in Kate's life.

He had been reading the monthly client reports at home one evening when he'd seen her name. A combination of fear and desire had broken through his whole body. He'd called the Boston lawyer assigned to the case and confirmed it was his Katie being described. Without hesitation he'd released the other lawyer from the case and arranged to handle it personally. He had never once considered the ramifications of their reunion.

"Did you pick this case because of me?" she asked, her shrewd intelligence piecing together what he wasn't saying.

"Yes." He knew better than to lie to her but also wasn't willing to offer her any more of an explanation for his actions.

Matt had been raised to be responsible, with the high expectations and demands of his family behind his every decision and action. He hadn't realized he resented it or what a heavy burden it was until he'd met Kate.

She'd never asked him for anything and in return she had been the first person in his life that Matt had wanted to do things for, simply to make her happy, to make her smile. This was in stark contrast to his family, who had been blatant and demanding in their needs, wants and expectations. Kate had got more joy out of simple things than Matt had known was possible. Remembering how she took her coffee or asking about how her exam went had seemed to mean the world to her, and had been a far cry from the over-the-top and lavish gestures his family had expected.

He had been the best version of himself during his time with her. It hadn't been anything she had done or said, it had been all the things she hadn't done that had made him feel a sense of freedom and a willingness to give of himself that he had never experienced. She'd had no expectations or demands of him and had never pushed for more than he'd offered.

It was that part of Kate that was driving his need to personally defend her, not his guilt, he told himself. She seemed to take in his answer, an internal debate apparent in the emotions that crossed her face before she let the matter drop.

He took her cue and refocused on the case. "Kate, I want you to think back to that night and the interactions you had with Mr. Weber and his family. Can you think of anything you said or did that would make the Webers believe there was negligence involved in his death?"

She was silent across the table, but her nonverbal cues made up for the lack of words. She tangled her hair into a knot, pulling it from her face as her perfect posture slouched in defeat. "Yes."

"What happened?" He knew the answer. He rarely asked a question without knowing the answer but he needed to hear it from her, even though he knew it would kill her to say it.

"I cried." No emotion was in her words, just a statement of fact. But the look on her face told a different story.

"When did you cry, Kate?" Memories of the two times he had ever seen Kate cry revolved in his mind. Both instances had been extreme, when she had been pushed to her limit.

"When I was talking to Mrs. Weber after her husband died." Still no elaboration. He hated this. Hated that his job was to force her to discuss something she had no desire to share with him. It went against everything they had once been.

"I need you to tell me exactly what happened." She stared at him and he couldn't tell what she was thinking. Minutes went by and he started to worry she would refuse him. Not for the first time he reconsidered whether he should be representing Kate, or whether the past between them was too much to overcome.

Finally she sighed, obviously resigning herself to the situation. "After Mr. Weber died, Tate, as the attending surgeon, went to talk to Mrs. Weber to disclose his death. When he was done I joined her in the operating room's family room. I had met her earlier in the night and felt compelled to see her. She already knew her husband was dead and was crying alone in the room when I got there. When she saw me she reached for me and I let her embrace me, and she didn't let go. The more she cried, the harder she held me. Eventually I started to cry too and I told her I was sorry."

"What were you sorry for, Kate?"

"I was sorry that she had lost the love of her life. That she was going to have to go on by herself and try to make a life without the one person she was meant to be with."

"Do you think it's possible that she misinterpreted your empathy as guilt?"

"Given that we are talking about it, I would say yes, wouldn't you?" Her derision was very clearly focused on herself, despite the sarcasm in her response.

Yes, he would. Kate crying and saying she was sorry would definitely raise suspicions when reflected on after the fact.

"Are there any other patients, nurses, or colleagues that would speak for a pattern of behavior? That you frequently empathize with your patients and their emotions?"

"No. That was the first and only time I have lost my composure at work."

"Is there anyone else in your life who can testify to your emotional nature?" He was reaching, looking for some way to get her out of a situation that now seemed partially her own making.

Her face changed. Gone was the steely armor and replacing it was the same softness he recognized from the past. "You."

"Me what, Kate?"

"You are the only person who has ever seen me cry." Her words were a painful confession, but the information was just the opposite. It highlighted to him what he had always known. They had been something different, something special, something he should have held onto at all costs. He couldn't let those thoughts take over; he needed to keep his focus. He knew bringing up the past would be a sure way to make Kate retreat and he wasn't willing to lose another minute with the real her.

"What was different about that night?"

"I'm not sure." She raked her hand back through her hair and looked down at the table as if she would find the answer she was looking for in the grain of the wood. "She really loved him and he loved her. I saw it between them in the emergency department, true love. Then within hours it was gone and I couldn't put together what would happen next. She was so lost without him already and all I could remember was what it felt like to lose the person you love. I remembered that feeling and knew that my love and pain were only a tenth of what she was experiencing, and I didn't know how to help her."

The most remarkable woman he had ever met looked defeated and it was enough to break his resolve. He didn't stop to question whether she was referring to her mother, him, or Tate Reed in her memories of pain and loss. He rose from his chair and crossed around to her, the drive to hold her in his arms breaking through his common sense. She looked up as he drew her up from her chair, her lips parting in shock. He didn't mean to kiss her, his intent, brief as it had been, had been to comfort and hold her, but one look into the depths of her eyes and the sweet fullness of her lips was enough to change his mind.

It was an experience in contrasts. The softness of her lips to the hardness of his mouth; the surprise in her reaction to the deliberate intent that drove him; the sweetness within her to the ruthlessness of the man he had become. She didn't pull away and the small surrender drove him harder. He explored her, reminding his mind and body of the places he had once been and had never forgotten. His tongue teased hers while his hands roamed her body in his embrace. Her hands clung to him, grabbing handfuls of the fabric of his shirt until the moment was broken and he felt her step back from the kiss and push him away.

She was staring at him, her eyes wide. "You want me."

His arms were still holding her and he was unwilling to let her move further away. He also wanted to make it clear to her who she was with and who was responsible for the dilation of her pupils, her parted moist lips, and the points of her nipples, which were pressing against the fabric of her long-sleeved cotton shirt.

"Why?" she whispered, the word coming at the end of a gasp to find her breath.

"Why what?" His brain had been robbed of its blood supply and his ability to comprehend her question was inhibited by the physical desire he was struggling to restrain.

"Why are you really back?" It was the question that had been in the background of their every interaction and had remained unasked and unanswered between them.

"Code Orange. Code Orange, Emergency Department. All available personnel." The hospital intercom sounded within the room, the intrusion startling both of them. His arms dropped and she moved away. He had no idea what the announcement meant, but as he watched her face change from the intimacy of her question to immediate business, he realized it was serious.

"That's a mass casualty code. I need to go." She went back to her spot at the table, shoved her textbook into her shoulder bag and then left without another look at him.

He was torn between anger at the interruption and relief that he didn't have to answer the question he didn't have an answer for.

He knew why he had left her but had no explanation for why he was back. He paced around the room, the motion helping him to organize his thoughts. It wasn't the first time he had thought it through. It was an argument he had had over and over again, and never once had he come to a different conclusion. Kate was special. She was beautiful, selfless, and genuine in her feelings and actions. She was everything he wanted and he had loved her enough to let her go before his world ruined her and robbed her of everything that made her the woman he loved.

Why was he back? He had asked himself a thousand times since coming to Boston. Why, after nine years of being apart, had he finally given in to the temptation to return to her? It wasn't that he had forgotten her. In the beginning it had taken every ounce of his willpower to break away from her. When she'd called and emailed he had forced himself to erase the messages before listening to or reading her words.

He had begun filling his life with women and alcohol, neither providing any comfort. For a time he'd actually thought he was losing his mind, because out of the corner of his eye he would think that he saw her across campus or heard her voice in a crowd. One afternoon he had walked into a campus coffeehouse and seen a woman that could have been her. The long brown hair, the way she had been bent over a textbook, intensely concentrating, reminding him so much of Katie that when she had started to look up he'd had to turn and leave. He had been unable to face the crushing disappointment that would have come when he discovered it was not her.

After that he realized he needed something in his life that reminded him of her without being with her. That was when he discovered medical defense law. It brought out the best in him, just as Kate had. The ability to defend and protect physicians who dedicated their lives to caring for others brought a purpose to his life that he desperately needed. It was also the first step in breaking free of his family's self-serving dysfunction.

After finishing law school, it had been understood that he would join the firm and he did, but with one condition—he wanted to specialize in medical defense. When faced with the prospect of having his grandson work for another law firm, his grandfather relented and let him start a separate division for medical defense within the family firm. Matt was the best at everything he did, but as a medical defense lawyer he excelled. Within two years the firm's value had tripled and Matt was made a partner. By twenty-eight, Matt was a millionaire, having channeled his share of the firm's profits into successful investments.

Despite being born into privilege, Matt became a self-made man, and with that came insight into the family dynamic that had dominated his life. He loved his family, but that feeling was marred by the sense of responsibility he felt toward them and disdain for their way of life. They judged and treated people entirely according to wealth and background with no regard for true character. They would have eaten the old Katie alive, and Matt knew that, despite his best efforts to protect her, his family's resentment of who she was and her position of importance in Matt's life would have slowly eroded her spirit and the small amount of self-confidence she had.

But now things were different. New money was no longer vulgar, not when Matt had accumulated more wealth than the rest of his family combined. He had also learned to draw some hard lines surrounding his personal life and they no longer dared to interfere in his relationships or other choices.

If his ability to control his family was the reason he was back in Kate's life, he would have found her years ago. He could more easily explain why he'd stayed away than why he'd returned. He'd stayed away out of guilt. No matter how noble his reasons had been for ending their relationship, he had done it horribly, his mind re-acting instead of thinking.

To avoid her sacrificing who she was and wanted to be for him, he had sacrificed his own character. He had stayed away because after all these years he knew he couldn't offer her what they had once had—trust. If she asked him again why he was back, he would be honest. He was back because she needed him and after nine years apart he finally had something to offer her, and he wasn't going to let her refuse.

CHAPTER FIVE

KATE REACHED THE emergency department within minutes of hearing the overhead call for help. A code orange was one of the most rare codes and in her entire career she had never heard one called. A code blue was called when a patient stopped breathing. A code red when there was a fire in the hospital. A code orange was reserved for when some sort of disaster occurred and the emergency department was overwhelmed and unable to cope with the patient load.

She wasn't working, she wasn't even supposed to be in the building, but that didn't matter. She had been trained to care for the sick and no office hours applied to that duty.

She threw her bag into the locker room, exchanging her shirt for a scrub top, not so much to protect herself but more to identify her in the sea of people that would be filling the department.

She walked to the trauma bay, coming alongside Chloe and her attending physician, Dr. Ryan Callum. They showed no surprise at her arrival.

"What's going on?" she asked, her eyes darting around the department, evaluating.

"Multiple vehicle collision in the tunnel, including a city bus, with an unknown number of casualties. The

Boston fire department and medics have been on scene for at least fifteen minutes but they are having trouble extracting some of the passengers. We are the closest and the first-response site for all trauma cases, with County and other surrounding hospitals as overflow."

"What would you like me to do?"

"The operating room has been notified and all non-urgent cases are on hold until we evaluate how much surgical trauma there is. Chloe and the other emergency residents are going to triage the victims according to their injury severity score. If you could be on hand for the critical and severe patients and work with the trauma team to decide who goes to the operating room and in what order, that would help immensely." He didn't elaborate further as the team poured into the ambulance bay to meet the first arriving victims.

Within an hour, fifteen patients had been classified with severe and critical codes. Kate mentally ordered the surgical cases for the operating room, taking into account both the severity of their injuries and their readiness for the operating room. She picked up the phone and asked to be put through to the attending surgeon responsible for the trauma team.

"Jonathan Carter," the surgeon answered, obviously waiting for this call.

"It's Kate Spence. I have seen the critical and severe tracked patients from the tunnel accident. Nine are presenting as clear surgical cases and four need to go immediately. There is an obstructed airway, a rib fracture with flail chest, a compound femur fracture, and a penetrating trauma to the abdomen."

"The operating room has four rooms available with nursing and anesthesia. Orthopedics has a team in place and can start with the femur and work through the orthopedics cases. I'm here and so is Dr. Reed, but we don't have a third surgeon in-house on a Saturday and the nearest person is one hour away because of the tunnel closure."

"Are you asking me which two of the three non-orthopedic cases we should take first?" she asked, knowing the wrong choice could lead to a patient's death.

"No, I'm telling you that you are taking the penetrating abdominal wound to the OR without an attending surgeon."

Her train of thought changed from patient triage to shock. She didn't need him to repeat himself; he had been clear and his words were echoing in her mind.

"Dr. Spence, you are three months away from being a board qualified surgeon. I've worked with you, Dr. Reed has worked with you, and we both agree that you are more than capable of acting alone. The patient is better served with you now than waiting around for someone else."

"Thank you." She felt humbled and terrified and neither emotion was she going to allow to show in her voice.

"Don't thank me. You've earned this. I've already notified the operating room that you will be doing the case solo. They are just waiting for the patient details and then will send for the patient immediately."

The team moved quickly. She made the necessary call and then went upstairs to change into her surgical attire. Within ten minutes the patient was on the table, being anesthetized. She moved to the left-hand side of the table and waited for the signal from the anesthetist to start. She could hear the monitors firing, her patient's heart rate racing, just as hers was. She knew she could do it. Knew they wouldn't have let her if she couldn't.

But there was something about being the most qualified person in the room, with no one to help her if she got in over her head, that was terrifying.

She needed to set the tone. Everyone in the room was on edge because of the severity of the situation. The only way to bring people down was to lead by example, to stay calm. She could do that. She held out her gloved hand. "Knife."

She worked meticulously, creating an incision extending from either side of the metal shard that was plunged into the center of the man's abdomen. She couldn't just pull it out, she needed the shard in place to act as a tamponade for the bleeding until she could identify which organs and vessels had been damaged. She worked through the layers of the abdominal wall until she was able to place a retractor to hold open the wound and give her the complete visualization she needed.

Damn, she thought to herself. The metal was extending into the transverse colon and the abdomen was completely contaminated, placing the patient at high risk for postoperative infection. Thankfully, the shard had stopped before reaching the aorta, which lay two centimeters below the tip.

Typically this was when her attending would ask her what she wanted to do. Did she want to repair the bowel or remove a segment of the damaged bowel, and if she chose the latter, did she want to do a primary or secondary repair? She knew the answer, but this was the first time she was taking one hundred percent ownership of the decision.

She called out to the circulating nurse and requested the necessary staplers and devices. Within an hour she was sitting in the recovery room with her patient, completing her postoperative orders and dictation.

Her emotions were mixed. On one hand she was proud of her surgical accomplishment; on the other, she felt for her patient, who still had a long road ahead of him to full recovery.

The automatic doors swung open and Dr. Carter walked in alongside the stretcher on which his patient was being transferred to the recovery room. He approached Kate, and she prepared to defend her decision to resect the bowel with delayed anastomosis.

"Dr. Shepherd has just arrived and is going to take over the third room until things are clear. Thank you for your help today. Your patient has been formally admitted under my care, but you should consider him yours until he goes home."

"Thank you again."

"Don't thank me. You proved yourself long ago."

She retraced her steps through the hospital, collecting her belongings from the various locations she had been. She had never questioned her decision to become a surgeon but in that moment she had never been more certain that she had made the right choice. She felt like the doctor and woman she wanted to be, confident and in control, and it was time for her to take control of all aspects of her life.

She dug through her bag in search of her phone and the business card the hospital's lawyer, Jeff Sutherland, had left her after the initial meeting. She dialed the number and waited as it rang.

"McKayne."

"It's Kate. We need to talk." It was the understatement of the year, but what she needed to say she needed to say in person. She wasn't going to take the easy way out over the phone.

"I won't dispute that." His assuredness irritated her and she tried to stay on track.

"Where are you now?"

"I'm at my apartment—do you need the address?" Yes, she would need the address. Leaving a man's apartment at three in the morning after an unexpected sexual encounter did not typically lend itself to remembering logistics, but it did remind her of the dangers of entering a lion's den.

"No. I mean I don't need the address because I'm not coming over. Can you meet me at Gathering Grounds on Beacon Street?" She held her breath, waiting for his response.

"I can probably be there in about an hour."

"Okay. I'll see you then." She pushed the off button, not wanting to prolong the conversation. She needed to keep every ounce of the confidence she had gained this afternoon for when she met Matt.

Almost exactly an hour later Matt entered the coffee shop. She knew he was there the moment he walked through the door, and she watched him get a coffee and then join her at her table.

"We need to speak quietly while we're talking about the case."

"I don't want to talk about the case," she said, still quietly, her personal life just as confidential to her as the details of the lawsuit.

"Okay, so what do you want to talk about?"

"Us."

"You said you didn't want to discuss the past."

"I don't. I want to make things clear now."

"Kate, nothing is more clear. You want me and I want you."

He was right. She wouldn't deny it. How could she when he had witnessed her response to him? Even as he spoke the words her body flushed with the memory of him. She swallowed hard and forced herself to remain focused. "That doesn't matter."

"How can it not matter that every time we touch, neither of us can keep control?"

"Because I can keep control, Matt. I don't know you, I never did. But I remember what it feels like to be hurt by you and those memories are way stronger than any physical attraction that still lingers between us."

His face, which had been heated describing the passion between them, cooled, and she faced a steely expression before he spoke. "Do you want a different lawyer?"

"No. You need to fix this for me, because I know you can. But while you are doing that I want you to forget everything else that is between us. The only relationship we have is of lawyer and client."

"The attraction between us isn't going away, Kate, no matter how hard you try to control it or tell me to ignore it."

"But you are, Matt. When this case is done you are going to move on back to your high-society life and you'll forget that I ever existed."

"And what if I can't?"

"You can, Matt, and you have. You just need to do it again."

Kate spent the remainder of the weekend trying to get caught up with life. Her work schedule made even basic life tasks seem like monumental challenges. Cleaning her apartment, doing laundry, shopping for groceries, and sorting her mail were all luxuries saved up for a

rare day off. Her student-loan statement was a grim reminder of the ruin she faced if they lost the case. She
had no way to pay back that amount of debt, not to
mention the money she owed her father, unless she was
employed as a surgeon, and that was dependent on the
case. Not to mention the pain of losing her chance to
devote her career to women with breast cancer, women
like her mother.

She moved through the apartment, trying to restore
the same order to her home life as she had her personal
life, and eventually she felt more herself than she had
since Matt's return. She had done it. She had taken the
steps she needed to protect herself and her heart. She
would never let him hurt her again, because if she did
she knew she wouldn't survive it.

Her sense of peace remained with her until Monday
afternoon. Matt's office called and scheduled a meeting
for Thursday. The receptionist didn't provide any details
about why they were meeting. She could only assume it
was to continue the conversation that had been cut short
on the weekend. Two feelings filled her and neither was
welcome. One was a sense of dread at having to relive
the night of Mr. Weber's death and her time with Mrs.
Weber. The other was hurt that Matt hadn't called her
himself. The latter she resented deeply, despite it being
what she wanted: lawyer and client, nothing more.

She operated all day Tuesday and took a call shift
on Wednesday in order to be able to leave early for the
meeting on Thursday afternoon. By that time her sense
of peace had long left her. It was just fatigue, she lied to
herself. That was why she felt so on edge about meeting
Matt, because she was in control and had every intention of staying that way.

"Kate, are you okay?" Tate's voice interrupted

her thoughts as she made her way through the hospital atrium towards the building's exit. It was jarring to hear his voice when she was thinking about Matt. She looked up to find him walking beside her, and she hadn't even noticed.

"I'm sorry, Tate, what did you say?"

"I asked if you were okay."

She wasn't going to lie to Tate. "No, but I am going to be," she said, with enough conviction to convince both of them.

"So where are you headed?" she asked as they left the hospital, his early departure as uncharacteristic as her own.

"I'm guessing the same place you are, to a meeting with Matt McKayne."

She shook her head from side to side, the momentary lightness now gone. Who was she kidding? The only person in control was Matt. He had always been in control, it was one of the things that had drawn her to him, but now she was terrified. If he was in control then she wasn't, and the small whisper of doubt she had over her ability to keep her emotional distance from him blossomed into fear.

"I don't think you have to worry about the lawsuit interfering with your fellowship. McKayne seems to know what he is doing."

Tate had assumed her anxiety was related to the lawsuit. She should have felt relieved at his assumption but instead she felt insulted. It felt like Tate was choosing Matt over her and it hurt. She couldn't help her bitter response. "Looks can be deceiving, Tate."

"You don't trust him," Tate replied, more as a statement than a question. Kate was glad they were walking, wanting to hide her face and blame her expression on the feel of the cold spring chill on her face.

"You do?" she countered, unwilling to divulge any information about whether or not she trusted Matt, because truthfully she still didn't know herself.

"Yes, I do. I am not sure what it is about him. He's arrogant and he likes to be in charge, but I can tell it comes from a driving need to succeed and do his job well. He probably should have been a surgeon."

"Ha," Kate scoffed, thinking about how Matt's family would have taken a departure from the legal profession.

"What is it you don't like about him?" Tate asked.

He broke my heart and abandoned me, Kate said inside her head. Out loud she simply said, "I think we are here."

They walked into the lobby of the downtown highrise and took the elevator to the top floor. Tate walked to the receptionist's desk to check in while Kate took in her surroundings. Matt had done well if the office was anything to go by. There were floor-to-ceiling windows with a view of the water. The office reception area was beautifully furnished with comfortable seating and a granite coffee bar. Tate handed her a warm mug. "I thought maybe you should avoid any more caffeine. It's lemon tea."

Kate looked down and noticed the small tremor in her hand that Tate had already taken note of. "Thanks."

"Dr. Spence and Dr. Reed."

She looked up and saw a middle-aged woman looking at her expectantly. Tate rose with Kate and they followed the woman through the open office area towards a corner office. "Mr. McKayne, Dr. Spence and Dr. Reed."

They walked into the office and sat in the two large leather chairs across from Matt's desk. Once seated, Kate took her first real glance at Matt. He was dressed in a charcoal-gray suit with a blue shirt and steel-gray tie that matched the cold look in his eyes. His jaw was clean-shaven and clenched. She couldn't read him and that bothered her on multiple levels.

"You went to Brown?" Kate turned to look at Tate, who was looking past Matt at his framed degree hanging on the wall behind the desk.

"Yes, I did my undergraduate degree there, before going to Columbia Law." She was watching Matt intently, waiting for him to change the focus and start discussing the case, but instead he was staring at Tate like she wasn't even in the room. He wouldn't, there was no way he would.

"Tate, as your lawyer, I need to disclose to you a potential conflict of interest I have in regard to this case."

"Go ahead, I'm listening."

Kate tried to speak, to stop Matt from saying whatever he was going to say, but no words came out.

"Kate and I knew each other during our undergraduate degree at Brown. We were lovers."

Everything was slipping away. She couldn't focus. Not on Matt, not on Tate, not even on her own thoughts and feelings that were racing through her. Cruel. This was cruel to her and to Tate. After what seemed like an eternity Tate's voice broke the silence.

"I would have appreciated that information much earlier. From Kate," Tate said in a monotone, turning his head towards her as he spoke. It was the same look he had worn the night they had broken up, one of shock and disappointment. She wouldn't look away, he deserved her attention, but maintaining eye contact did nothing to assuage her feelings of helplessness and shame. He was right: he had deserved the truth from her.

"Tate, I can explain," she said, knowing nothing was going to make this better. She had already destroyed their relationship once, and just when they were finally getting back on track with being the friends they always should have just been, she had lied to him and allowed him to be made a fool of in front of Matt.

"You don't need to explain anything to me, Kate. Your sexual relationships are no longer relevant to me, but I thought we were going to be honest with each other from here on in. I guess I was wrong." He rose from the chair and turned, focusing his attention on Matt.

"Matt, at this point there is only one thing I want from you. I want this case and my connection to Kate over." Then he walked out of the room, and the sound of the door slamming behind her made her jump.

"Kate, I had to tell him," she heard Matt saying from across the desk with an air of authority and conviction that she didn't appreciate. His tone only helped to fuel the deep sense of hurt that had been close to the surface since their reunion and now was ready to boil over.

"You have to do a lot of things, Matt. You have to be the perfect son, the perfect grandson, and now the perfect lawyer. But what you really are is the perfect coward, taking the easy way out, hiding behind all the grandiose responsibilities of your perfect, rich, high-society life, ignoring the real things in life you have to be responsible for."

"What are you talking about, Kate?" He hadn't yelled, but he might have, to look at him. Still, the look of Matt, his jaw clenched, his hands gripping the arms of his chair was not enough to stop the words that she had screamed in her head for years.

"That's just it, Matt, you are so screwed up that you still haven't bothered to figure out what is really important to you."

"And Tate Reed? That is who's important to you these days, is it, Kate?" He had left his chair, his hands bracing his body as he leaned across the desk towards her. Even though they were still feet apart, she felt him, his anger, his fire, and she drew back in her chair, pressing herself into the back of it.

"Yes, Matt. My friends are important to me and they deserve to be treated far better than what Tate got today."

"You don't think Tate deserved to know we were lovers?" His words were sarcastic, and everything about him reminded her of a hunter about to go in for his final attack, but she wasn't about to concede to him now.

"We were never lovers, Matt. You never loved me. You may not remember that, but I do."

She stood from the chair and was happy that she had kept her coat with her, feeling more than ready to leave this conversation and Matt's office. She had turned towards the door when she felt Matt grab her hand and spin her back towards him.

"Kate, don't go, we're not done," he ordered.

Grief tore through her and settled low in her stomach. "I didn't go, Matt, you did. I trusted you once and I was wrong, and I have had to live with that. But we are done, Matt. You decided that years ago." She backed away and he let her go.

She walked into the dimly lit establishment that was filled with the rich smell of wood and the sound of fiddle music playing in the background. Her eyes scanned the room until she found what she was looking for.

She went to the bar, ordered two eighteen-year-old single malt Scotches, and walked over to Tate's booth, sliding in on the leather padded bench opposite and passing over the tumbler before he took notice.

"I should have told you about my past with Matt. I was wrong and you have every right not to forgive me, but I really hope you do because you are one of the few people in this world that I trust and I respect so much more than my actions have shown." Her words tumbled from her with unmistakable sincerity.

"You have always had more guts than any other surgeon I know." He picked up the glass she had brought him and took a fortifying mouthful. "That night six months ago you were right."

"I know. We both did everything we could to save Mr. Weber but it was futile."

Tate shook his head. "No, Kate, you were right about us. We were great friends and we loved each other, but we were not *in love* with each other. It took me a long time to admit that to myself. My pride was hurt when you rejected my proposal and the anger I felt towards you made it hard for me to realize that I was more angry than sad at what should have been the loss of the love of my life but wasn't."

"And now?" Kate asked tentatively, not knowing where the conversation was going.

"Now I should probably thank you and apologize to you for being an ass for the past several months, including my part in what happened today."

"You have every right to be angry about what happened today. I'm angry. I should have been honest with you from the start when you asked if Matt and I knew each other. But it wasn't like how he made it sound."

"It doesn't matter. For the most part, what happened in your past is none of my business."

"For the most part?"

"Unfortunately, he is our hospital-appointed lawyer, and requesting a change in counsel might bring to light this little love triangle that I think we all would like to keep under wraps."

"The hospital rumor mill would love that. It would give the operating room nurses something to gossip about well after my departure. Kate Spence, surgical slut."

"Don't." For the first time in the conversation Tate's anger returned. "You and I both know you are absolutely anything but."

"Thank you," she replied, embarrassed. Despite her level of comfort with Tate, it was still awkward to discuss her sexual history, particularly as he represented half of her total number of partners. He must have felt the same, because he drained the remainder of his glass.

"He still has feelings for you." Kate's eyes flew wide and landed on Tate. "It took me a while to pick up on it because things were so tense and uncomfortable between us, but today at his office I think he was clearly marking what he considers his."

"I'm not his, he never wanted me. He made that very clear, repeatedly clear."

Tate's face quirked sarcastically and he changed his voice to a slow,, explanatory drawl. "Kate, I think we have already delicately established that at one time he wanted you very much, and I'm not wrong about him now. Finish your drink and let's get out of here. We both have early mornings."

Outside the bar he hailed them a cab and rode with her back to her apartment. When the cab stopped she immediately saw Matt sitting on the front steps of the brownstone, waiting.

"You have company. Do you want me to leave?" Tate asked as the cab pulled to a stop.

"No," she responded, not sure what she wanted to happen but knowing she was in no state to be alone with Matt. Outside his office, out of his expensive suit, he looked more like the Matt she'd known, and she still didn't trust herself, angry or not, to be with him.

Without further words, Tate paid the driver and exited the vehicle, coming around to her side to open the door and secure an arm around her waist both for support and as a statement.

"McKayne," Tate greeted Matt.

"Reed," Matt replied, before turning his burning stare directly to Kate. "I need to talk to you."

"We have already talked today and we both said what we wanted to say. Nothing has changed since then."

"By the looks of things, a lot has changed since then."

"Not between you and I. Now, if you will excuse us, it's late." Kate avoided any further eye contact as she brushed past him, but felt his anger. She opened the door to her building and eventually the one to her apartment, with Tate still behind her. She didn't look back when the door closed.

"He's gone." Tate answered her unasked question. "And I'm not wrong. Matt wants you. Badly." There was no jealousy in his words.

"'Night, Kate. Take care of yourself." Then he turned and left. Kate walked over to the door and locked up for the night. If only keeping her heart safe from Matt McKayne was that easy.

CHAPTER SIX

KATE WAS BACK with Tate. Again the sound of their names together and the very thought of it was sickening. Apparently competition was all Tate had needed to see the light and reclaim Kate as his own, and she had been ready and willing. He walked to the kitchen bar and poured himself a drink. He took a sip, allowing the feeling of the cool liquid flowing down his throat to replace the taste of bile the image Kate with another man brought forth.

It didn't help. He reached for his keys on the entry table but then common sense returned. Nothing good would come of going back to Kate's tonight. It would probably have the opposite effect of pushing Kate further into the other man's arms. But he needed to do something. Something to take his mind away from the jealousy he felt towards Tate and the anger he felt towards himself for ever letting her go. He dropped the keys back onto the table, peeled off his shirt and went towards the punching bag in the den. Not bothering to change out of his jeans, he hit the bag, once, twice, and then again and again. No matter how many times or how hard he hit the bag, nothing changed. He wasn't the man in Kate's life any more, and he was entirely responsible for that.

He stopped punching and ran his hand through his sweat-drenched hair, feeling his chest rise and fall with the force of his exertion. He needed to cool off his body and his temper so he walked outside onto the penthouse balcony, letting the cold night air hit the bare skin of his chest. He rested his hands on the cement ledge, looking out into the night and without thought in the direction of Kate's apartment. He couldn't escape it. Tonight was going to be another night where he relived their ending and the choice he had made.

Kate had always been a temptation he couldn't resist. From the moment he'd seen her, to every time he had spent time with her, he had told himself he needed to walk away, until he finally had, but not until after the damage had already been done.

If he had known how they were going to end, maybe that would have been enough to keep him from her. But from the moment he'd met her she had became like a vice, a secret addiction that he felt powerless against. He had known that it would never last, couldn't last. Kate hadn't fitted into his world, and the way they had been together wouldn't have lasted once his real life had intruded.

The end was supposed to be graduation. Kate had applied to several medical schools, but of all the Ivy League schools that had accepted her, only Boston had provided her the scholarship she had needed to be able to attend. She'd had no choice: if she wanted to be a doctor then Boston was it. For the complete opposite reasons he'd had to go to New York. Every man in his family had attended Columbia Law and despite his ever-increasing resentment towards his family and their demands, he hadn't been able to abandon the tradition his own father had been a part of.

Their end came more spectacularly and painfully than he ever could have imagined. It was Kate's last night at Brown before she moved home for the summer. It was also their last night together. They had talked about visiting each other, staying in touch, but both knew their workloads and schedules were likely to make that impossible, no matter how much they wanted it to happen. He also knew that Kate was an indulgence he couldn't afford to keep, not with the life that was planned for him.

So that last night she came over to his apartment, like she always did, and they settled in for a night of the "usual." Take-out, beer and a movie that was meant to serve as a distraction from the inevitable goodbye. As the movie droned on in the background, as she had many times before, Katie cuddled into his side, her naturally cold hands tucked into the warmth of his body. Despite his attraction to her, he had never let their "friendship" become closer than this. What had become torture for him months ago now felt like a life-line slipping from his grasp.

He was never going to have this again, be with her again, and as he looked down at her, she tilted her head up to meet his gaze. Her eyes said everything he was feeling. This was it, this was their end, and her lips started to part. She was going to say goodbye, and he didn't want to hear it. He needed to stop her and instinct took over as he brought his mouth crashing down on hers.

Never in a million years would he have imagined the instant explosive desire he felt on contact with her lips. They were soft and pressed against his. Still partly open, he slid his tongue across them, tasting her; she gasped and he slid his tongue into her mouth, wanting more. He encircled her with his arm, his hand weaving into her hair to hold her against him. Then he felt it, the tentative motion of Katie tasting him back. He slowed for a moment, enjoying the feeling of her exploring him, before his desire was once again demanding more.

He pushed them both back across the couch, her body fitting perfectly beneath him. He moved from her lips to her cheek and down her neck, his body supported on one flexed arm, while his other hand dipped underneath her shirt and pressed into her bare abdomen. He heard her moan, felt her arch against him. More, he need more, and he rose from her long enough to pull both their shirts over their heads before coming back to her.

He continued where he'd left off, kissing her neck, her shoulders, her collarbone, and then the tops of her breasts, which were pushing out of her black lace bra. He brushed his hand over her breast, feeling her hard nipple jutting for attention. Then he cupped her and let his thumb trace the nipple's outline. More, his lips found the other nipple, and Katie gasped as he kissed and suckled through the black lace. She arched again and he reached behind her and undid the clasp. She grabbed the front of the bra and tugged herself free.

She was perfect. Her brown hair fanned over the couch, her eyes a sultry gray he had never seen before, and her creamy-white skin pink with a flush he now knew extended beyond her face.

He returned to her mouth and kissed her as deeply as he could. Her hands traced up his chest, then curled as she clung to him. She wanted him and he had to have her. He didn't stop kissing her as he reached for the button on her jeans, pulling them open. His hand slipped inside and he used the heel of his hand to grind against her. She gasped and then moved against him. It was all the encouragement he needed as he slipped his fingers inside to feel her. She felt like hot silk and for the first time Matt thought he might not be able to hold on as he felt himself getting harder than he had ever felt.

Opening his own jeans for relief, he then removed both pairs, pulling her small black panties with her jeans. He was staring at the most beautiful naked woman he had ever seen when Katie reached up and touched him. Her fingers first brushed against the length of him and then encircled him. Her thumb rubbed against the moistness at his tip. He couldn't wait or last any longer. He moved between her legs and reached behind her thigh to draw one leg up to open her to him and then plunged into her as deep and hard as he could.

He heard her cry out at the same time as he registered the exquisite tightness and muscles clamped all around him. He looked down and saw the pain across her face and a small tear coming from her eye. Oh, God, what had he done? He started to withdraw when her hands came up and grabbed his shoulders to hold him in place. "Don't move," she whimpered.

"Katie, I'm hurting you."

"Please, Matt, just don't move."

"Katie."

"Please," she begged.

Katie had never asked him for anything before this moment and he shuddered at the thought of this being her first request. He closed his eyes and buried his face in her neck as he tried to block out the reality that she was a virgin and he had hurt her. He took a deep breath, inhaling the rosemary and mint scent of her shampoo. He couldn't face the tears in her eyes right now, so instead he spoke softly into her ear.

"Katie, do you trust me?"

"Yes." The honesty in her response was heartbreaking.

"Okay, wrap your arms around my neck and hold onto me." She complied, and Matt reached behind her other thigh, holding her to him as he lifted them both into a sitting position, keeping himself deeply embedded within her but now with her in control. He ran his fingers softly up and down her bare back, trying to soothe the pain.

"I'm sorry," she cried softly.

"Shh… I'm the one who's sorry, Katie." His hand cupped her face and his thumb brushed away the few tears that were there. Then he kissed her softly and was rewarded with her kissing him back. How long they stayed locked together, kissing, exploring each other's mouths, tasting and trailing paths across each other's necks he didn't know, but he did notice the first small rise and fall of Katie against him. His body had not forgotten where it was and her small movement was enough to make him harden further.

"Oh," she gasped.

Before he could beg her to let him let go so he could stop hurting her, she moved again, a little more this time. This time the expression on her face was far from one of pain. She was mesmerizing as she moved up and down against him. Her hands anchored on his shoulders as he reached around and cupped her bottom. Each movement was slightly more than the last, her breathing becoming more erratic.

He removed one hand from her bottom and gently spread her, letting his fingers brush her swollen nub at the same time she moved against him. This time her cry was not of pain, and Matt felt her lean into him and increase her pace and depth. She was so tight that every time she moved he felt himself push into a new hot, wet place. Her movements also caused her breasts to brush against his chest with every stroke. Her bottom was firm beneath his hand and his other hand confirmed the wetness he was feeling from the inside.

It was only his fascination with watching her that kept him from losing control. Gently, Matt lifted his hips to meet her downward stroke. Then with each subsequent stroke she came down a little faster, a little harder, a little deeper as Matt continued to rise up to meet her. Then he heard her start to hold her breath, little cries escaping her throat, until she raised herself to his tip and came down as deep and hard as his first thrust, crying out, and he felt her shudder and pulsate against him. He gripped her hips, pulling her as hard to him as he could, and cried out with equal satisfaction as he emptied into her still pulsating body.

She was collapsed against him, panting and slick with sweat, when he heard her whisper, "I love you."

His heart had been pounding and his mind racing, trying to take in everything that had just happened. It was an impossible situation to avoid, with Katie wrapped around him, him still inside her. He had played with fire and had gotten burned. After over a year of resisting his attraction to her they had gone over a cliff together, past the point of no return. He tried to think rationally, which was almost impossible in the circumstances, but one of them had to, and apparently it wasn't going to be Katie. He had heard of women becoming emotionally attached to their first lovers, overwhelmed by the experience. Was that what she was feeling? Surely if Katie loved him she would have told him before this.

He wrapped his arms back around her and stood, still clutching her to him. He strode through to the bedroom, where he laid her on the bed, finally separating them. He was pained at the small stain of blood on her thigh, recalling the force that had put it there. He lay down beside her, drawing the duvet over both of them. Katie backed against him, her curves tucking against him, and without thought he wrapped his arm around her. "I'm sorry, I didn't know. Are you okay?" he asked quietly.

"I'm perfect," she responded softly, taking his hand in hers and nestling further into him. Minutes later she was asleep, her breathing the only sound in the dark quiet night.

He didn't sleep. He lay there tortured by the naked reminder of what they had done and tried to figure out where they would go from there. He stared at the night's lights through his bedroom window and played the arguments in his head over and over again. They had passed the point of no return, and the impossible task of saying goodbye to her had just gotten infinitely harder. It had been a night of firsts for both of them. Kate had lost her virginity and he had actually felt like they had made love, unlike his previous physical encounters. With the added emotion he had become out of control with desire and need. He couldn't think straight. Not with Katie naked, pressed against him. Not while he was hard and using all his energy just to resist waking her up to make love to her all over again.

When morning had come, he awoke to find Katie facing him, her eyes watching him intently. "I'm not going to Boston." She had been definitive in her statement and

Matt felt the ramifications of their night together growing beyond what he had lain awake imagining.

"Of course you are. I'm going to New York and you are going to Boston, Katie. You know that." He tried to keep the panic from his voice and match her decisiveness.

"I don't want to go to Boston, Matt. Not without you." The situation was spiraling out of control. Did she know what she was saying? Medical school, her scholarship, everything she had worked for, she was going to give that up? For him? No way in hell was he going to let that happen. He had spent his life not being able to have his own dreams or plans and he would be damned if Katie was going to give up hers. He got out of the bed and grabbed the nearest pair of jeans on the bedroom floor, wincing slightly as the denim covered his body's response to her nakedness.

In a single moment he knew what he needed to do and didn't stop to think before the words came from his mouth. "Katie, last night was a mistake." She recoiled and he could tell that he had hurt her, but if that was what it took to keep her from throwing her life away then so be it.

"I don't believe you." He could tell that she was trying to be brave with her tone and eye contact, but he also saw that she was now clutching the sheet in her fist as she clung to it. She was still so innocent and he wasn't going to let his family take that from her.

"I told you last night that I was sorry it happened." Even he wasn't sure at that moment whether he was telling the truth or not. Would he trade last night not to hurt her this morning? The only thing he did know was that he would not let her sacrifice her dreams for him.

"And I told you last night that I love you. And I think you love me too."

She was so brave and so beautiful, and at that moment he knew that he did love her, was in love with her, and loved her enough to do the right thing and let her go, by whatever means necessary.

"Katie, you don't love me. You just think you love me because of last night, because of it being your first time."

"Don't tell me what I think or how I feel, Matt. I loved you before last night, during last night, and even now."

"Katie, I'm sorry. I don't love you." And he turned and left the room, but not before he saw the look of pain strike as his words hit her. When he entered the living room, reminders of the previous night were all around. The half-eaten pizza, the couch cushions on the floor, their clothes haphazardly scattered across the room. He had to leave. He couldn't face any reminders of what they had shared, reminders that might make him weaken and change his mind, go back to her, tell her he loved her, let her sacrifice herself to be with him. He picked up his shirt, grabbed his keys and left without looking back. When he returned hours later the apartment was empty and Katie was gone.

CHAPTER SEVEN

A SLEEPLESS NIGHT turned into a painful morning as Matt arrived at his office. For the first time in his life he had arrived after eight and already regretted the time spent in self-recrimination over a past that he could not change. He walked through the waiting room on a direct route to his office and saw Tate stand and walk towards him.

"We need to talk," Tate said bluntly. He was looking him directly in the eye and was obviously not going to back down or be dissuaded.

"Not here," Matt replied, aware that there was potential for this conversation to end in the two men coming to blows, and wanting to keep that event out of the office. "I need a cup of coffee."

The two men walked out in silence and remained that way for the ten minutes it took them to reach a local coffee shop. They each ordered and sat down at a table, sizing up each other. Tate was not backing down in his gaze or the hard line of his jaw.

"Are you here to tell me to stay away from Kate?" Matt asked bluntly, challenging the man sitting opposite him.

"No. Kate is a grown woman who is capable of making her own decisions," Tate answered calmly. The man was confident, but Matt would be too if he had just come from Kate's bed.

"Apparently," he replied sarcastically. "So what do we need to talk about, then?"

"Whether you are the best person to be representing us," Tate answered in the same calm tone, unfazed by Matt's barb.

"I'm the best," Matt stated definitively. Through the long hours of last night he had questioned that very issue, wondering if he could stand being with Kate and the man who had taken his place throughout the duration of the case. In the end he'd decided to stay on the case because he still wanted the best for her, and he was still the best.

"I don't doubt that. My problem is that your former relationship with Kate and the unresolved issues between you are not compatible with working well together. You also probably do not have my best interests at the top of your list of priorities either." Tate was faintly smiling at his last comment.

"So you want me to resign from the case?" Matt asked, feeling no patience for whatever game the other man was playing.

"That was my first instinct. Then I realized that your resignation would lead to a lot of questions. The last thing I want is for anyone else to know about you and Kate." Any trace of a smile was gone and Matt saw anger in his eyes for the first time since his initial disclosure of their past together.

"Why is that? You don't like the comparison?" Matt knew he shouldn't be pushing, but he couldn't help himself, his burning resentment overtaking his well-practiced interview skills.

"What I don't want is the hospital administration

rumor mill circulating the exploits of Dr. Spence's sex life. She'll be portrayed as something we both know she's not."

Matt hated Tate at that moment, hated and respected him for putting Kate first. It was sickening to think that she might have replaced him with a man who was better and more worthy of her than him.

"So what do you want?" Matt finally responded.

"I want you to do your job. I want the lawsuit against us dropped so that we all can move on with our lives."

"And Kate?"

"I've said what I came here today to say. You can figure out the rest." Then he walked out, leaving Matt at the table.

How many casualties did an event have to involve before it was considered to be a mass trauma? Kate wondered. She was sitting in the café near her brownstone, studying for the board exam, and unfortunately drawing parallels between the state of her life and emergency states. Factor A, the man who had broken her heart. Factor B, a lawsuit threatening her career. Factor C, the risk of failing the board exam due to stress from the aforementioned factors A and B. For the first time in years she was distracted; the words she read fleeing her mind as soon as she read them.

She felt overwhelmed. This was not a new state for her as she was constantly overwhelmed by the physical and emotional strain of her job. But now, for the first time, she felt guilt towards Matt, and the mere presence of the new emotion was enough to push her past her tipping point. It was a struggle, feeling anger towards him and his nerve at coming back into her life as if he belonged there and on the other hand feeling guilt for

misleading him about the status of her relationship with
Tate. She didn't want to be the bad guy; she didn't want
to be anything. She wanted to let go of her relationship
with Matt; she just didn't know how to do that.

As if on cue, she lifted her eyes away from her textbook for the hundredth time that afternoon, but this time
they fell on Matt. He was walking towards her in jeans
and a black polo shirt, which made him look younger
than his expensive tailored suits did. The effect was
still the same, though, and she watched as several female heads turned and admired everything he had to
offer. It was odd that she never stopped being taken in
by his pure physical beauty. It wasn't just his tall stat-
ure, powerful build, or the face whose features aligned
perfectly, from his deep blue eyes to the perfect faint
pink lips that sat between the masculine jaw and nose.
It was him, his presence, the effortlessness he exuded.

This was not a made-up appearance, this was who
he was—a man like no other. She couldn't look away,
even when parts of her reacted treacherously, still apparently remembering the feel of and taste of him from
nights earlier.

Aside from unwanted attraction, she couldn't move
past the astonishment of watching Matt walk up to her
table and take a seat opposite her, so much like years
past that it hurt, and she swallowed the pain she felt
rising within her. She waited, speechless, to hear what
was going to come next. What else did they have to say
to each other? How much more pain could they cause
each other?

"Ask me how I found you?" It was more of a challenge than a question. He was resting on his forearms
on the table, his body leaning forward, his entire focus
on her.

"I don't know," she replied honestly, confused with where the conversation was going.

He reached over and pushed a lock of hair behind her ear, twirling it in his fingers before he uncovered her face. "Because, Kate, I know you."

"No, you don't." She lacked his conviction. His single touch had been less physically intimate than most of their contact since his return, but emotionally it tore at her resolve. He seemed to believe every word he was saying, but she still felt the need to contradict him, to protect herself from the temptation of him.

"Yes, Kate, I do. I appreciate and respect everything that you have accomplished, but that doesn't change who you are."

"Who am I, Matt?" She couldn't resist the question. It was a question that had plagued her for years. Who was she in his eyes?

"You're mine." His eyes flashed with the same possession his words held. She should have been offended, she should have been afraid, but what she felt was want.

"No." The word escaped her lips, but in truth it was more a reminder to herself of what she could not have.

"Yes, you are, Kate, you always have been. You and I both know that."

She had been his. She couldn't deny that she had been one hundred percent in her feelings towards him, so much so that the memory of their coming together still brought with it as much a memory of completeness as it did emotional pain. She had also never given him up, not completely, not enough to move on and fall in love with someone else. Enough was enough, though. She wasn't going to let him keep playing whatever game he was playing.

"What do you want, Matt?"

"Isn't it obvious? I want you."

"It's too late, Matt, you can't have me." Nothing changed in his demeanor, except that he appeared even more focused and more all-encompassing. He had heard her, but obviously didn't believe her.

"I already have you, Kate, and this time I have no intention of walking away. The sooner you accept that, the sooner we'll all be better off."

Then, without warning, he stood over the table, leaned down and pressed his lips to her forehead. This time he lingered. She could smell his cologne, breathed in his scent, and felt that heat of his body, before he pulled away. Then, just as he had joined her, he turned and left.

Shock seeped through her from her forehead, which he had kissed so sweetly, to all the muscles inside her that contracted at his touch. Several parts of their conversation competed for attention in her mind. Had he remembered the night she had cried about her mother and he had kissed her on the forehead after carrying her to bed, the night she had realized she was in love with him?

Then there were his words, not just the words but the way he had said them. He had left no room for doubt that he had meant everything he had said. But would she know if he hadn't? She had spent her career learning to trust herself and her instincts, but with Matt she couldn't trust herself, her feelings, or him. All the words, declarations, and touches couldn't change the words that had been carved into her soul. "Katie, I'm sorry. I don't love you."

The offensive wail of her pager broke through her thoughts and provided temporary respite. She dialed the hospital operator and was patched through to the emergency department. Within a minute she was gone from the shop, her focus back where it needed to be and the past left behind.

CHAPTER EIGHT

She reached the hospital within fifteen minutes and was in the trauma room gowned and shielded before the ambulance arrived. Chloe was standing next to her, both women waiting. This time their entire interaction was succinct and directed towards patient care.

The ambulance attendants rolled a gurney into the trauma room and the patient was transferred to the hospital bed. The young man appeared to be in his early twenties and was strapped to a backboard with full C-spine precautions. Chloe took the head of the bed and assessed his airway and level of consciousness while he was hooked up to monitors, and Kate and the trauma-team nurses completed a full body survey, assessing for areas of maximal trauma and prioritizing injuries for care.

"His airway is compromised and GCS is six—we need to intubate," Kate heard Chloe order. And for a window of ninety seconds the team stood back while Chloe intubated the young man. After the endotracheal tube was in place, she and Kate auscultated the lung fields. She didn't hear any breath sounds on the right, and Chloe confirmed the finding.

"Set up for a chest tube," Kate called. A sterile tray of instruments was opened and after quickly prepping the skin and changing into sterile gloves, she made a stab incision above one of the man's ribs and inserted the hard plastic tube until she felt a loss of resistance and heard the trapped air escaping, allowing the man's lung to reinflate.

"Breath sounds on the right established. Good job, Kate," Chloe said.

Once the patient's airway, breathing and circulation had been stabilized, Kate continued. "Details," she called to the paramedic team, who remained in the room.

"Unknown male, traveling by bicycle when he was hit at moderate speed by a mid-sized SUV. The patient was found several yards from his bicycle, with his helmet still in place but cracked in multiple locations."

"Has he been conscious since your team arrived?"

"No."

"Chloe, once you're happy he's stable for movement, we need to move for a full-body CT. I need to know what to worry about first, blood in his brain or blood in his chest and belly."

"He should be stable enough in five minutes. He needs more volume so that he can maintain his pressure and make up for any ongoing losses prior to going to the operating room."

"Okay. I'm going to call the OR now and have them set up. Have the team page me once his scans are done so I can review them immediately with the in-house radiologist."

"Will do."

"Thanks."

Four hours later, Kate was finally leaving the intensive care unit, where she had just dropped off her patient di-

rect from the operating room. She was still strapped to
her pager as the trauma team leader for the week, but
now had a momentary reprieve. The cyclist's helmet had
saved his life. His brain had fared okay in the collision.

Unfortunately, the same could not have been said
for his spleen, which had suffered a massive laceration
after he had hit the curb. The young man had needed
an emergency laparotomy and splenectomy, along with
several units of blood and blood products, but was going
to recover.

Kate walked back to the emergency department to
find Chloe finishing up the paperwork from a shift
that should have ended an hour and a half earlier. Kate
hadn't bothered to change out of her scrubs and the
clogs she'd worn in the operating room and felt exhausted from the fast pace and physical demands of the
procedure. Chloe looked like she felt the same, appear-
ing pale in contrast to her bright red hair and the dark
blue of the hospital scrubs the emergency doctors also
wore. Kate slumped into the chair beside her friend,
losing her normal good posture.

"He's okay. It was a spleen trauma, but it's out and
he's stable in the intensive care unit," Kate reported,
knowing Chloe's desire to follow all of her patients.

"Thanks for coming back and letting me know."

Chloe stood from her chair and wavered before
reaching down to the desk for support.

"Are you okay, Chloe?" Kate asked.

"Yeah, just tired, stressed, busy, the usual. I think
I might have some low-grade virus or something that
has pushed me over the edge."

"Is there anything I can do?" Kate asked, concerned
that for the first time her perfectly put-together friend
was actually admitting to struggling. Chloe had al-

ways made everything seem effortless, which made Kate worry that she was feeling a lot worse than she was admitting.

"Don't you think you have enough on your plate?" Chloe asked, one eyebrow arching upwards, in a friendly, teasing tone.

"More than I ever wanted, but I'm sorting through it the best I can." She stared at Chloe, knowing what she should say but fighting a lifelong instinct to keep things inside. "I know that you're tired, but I was wondering if I could drive you home and maybe we could talk a bit."

Chloe stopped all the other tasks she was trying to finish and looked Kate in the eye. "That would be more than okay. Give me ten minutes to hand over my patients and I'll meet you by the parkade elevators."

True to her word, Chloe met her and they managed their escape without further interruption. "Are you hungry?" Kate asked, realizing she had missed lunch and supper while dealing with the trauma.

"A little bit. Do you have anything at your house?"

"No. Do you?"

"No. Eating out, it is."

Creatures of habit, Kate and Chloe tucked themselves into the back of the small Italian restaurant where the staff knew them by name. Kate waited to order and for their drinks to arrive before she drew in a breath and took the plunge. "Matt wants me."

Chloe didn't appear surprised. "What does that mean exactly?"

"I have no idea. At first it seemed purely physical and I thought you were right about it stemming from jealousy over Tate, and I told him that I wanted nothing more than a lawyer-client relationship. Then he told Tate about our past and we had a huge fight, which didn't seem to deter him at all because he showed up again today."

"And?"

"He said I was his and that I always have been and I always would be." She shivered, saying his words aloud having no less impact than hearing them from him hours earlier.

"Is he right?"

"I don't know. I don't understand what happened between us all those years ago and I don't understand what's happening now."

"So stop trying to think through and understand everything. How do you *feel*, Kate?"

"Terrified."

"What are you terrified of?"

"Of trusting him. Of making the same mistakes, getting hurt and losing myself all over again."

"Okay, that's a start. If you could trust him and weren't going to get hurt, would you want to be with him?"

"Yes."

"Are you still in love with him?"

"Yes." She was surprised at how quickly the words left her, but knew in the instant she heard her own answer that it was the truth.

"Can you talk me through what happened last time?"

"He was my everything. We met in my third year of undergraduate studies at Brown and became friends. He still had a long-distance girlfriend back in New York. During our friendship I fell in love with him, but never told him or acted on my feelings. After graduation he was going to law school in New York and I had a full scholarship to medical school in Boston."

"So what changed things?"

"Our last night together was unbearable. It was the end: he was going to go on with his life and me with mine. I spent the evening torn between telling him I loved him and just saying goodbye. Then before I said anything he kissed me."

"And?"

"And I thought we made love."

"I'm confused."

"We had sex. I told him I loved him and fell asleep in his arms happier than I had ever been in my entire life. The next morning I knew I couldn't say goodbye and I told him I wasn't going to."

"And?"

"He said he didn't love me and it had been a mistake. Then he went back to New York to be with his girlfriend and I never heard from him again."

"Oh, my God, Kate, I'm so sorry. I can't even imagine how devastating that must have been."

"What's worse is that I didn't believe him at first. After he left I waited for him to come back to apologize, to tell me the truth, that he loved me and things were going to be okay. But he never came back. I sat in his apartment for hours, waiting, hoping, and he never came back. Even after I left his apartment, I still thought he just needed time, that there was no way he could touch and hold me the way he had and not be in love with me too."

"So what did you do?"

"I held on as long as I could. I gave up my scholarship to Boston and managed to secure a place at Columbia in New York. I begged my father to take a second mortgage on our house to cover the lost scholarship and I left messages for Matt to tell him I was in New York when he was ready to talk."

"He never tried to contact you?"

"No, he never looked back. I believed in him so much that I lost all faith in myself."

The waitress arrived with their order and Kate was grateful for the interruption. As cathartic as it felt to finally talk about what had happened, it also brought to the surface how she had felt.

Both women were silent as they began to eat. Kate's mind kept telling herself the story. Matt's abandonment had left her with a small seed of self-doubt that had germinated over months of loneliness. She hadn't been able to resist following the coverage of his life in the society pages, and seeing him with other women had intensified her loneliness.

It had been a cold, windy day in November when she'd seen him again, walking across campus. She hadn't seen him in five months but had recognized him instantly in the crowd. She'd called his name and he'd turned to look and then kept walking. She'd convinced herself that he hadn't seen her. The second time she'd seen him she'd called his name more loudly and he'd moved his head slightly in her direction but hadn't turned around.

The final rejection had come in March. She had been sitting in a local coffee shop, studying, determined to make the dean's honor list so she would qualify for a scholarship the following year. She had been deep in thought when she'd had a sense that she hadn't felt in almost a year. She'd looked up and seen Matt, the same old Matt, in jeans and a cream sweater, with his brown leather tote bag slung across one shoulder. She'd seen him as he'd been looking at her and turning away.

That time she hadn't been able to say anything, she hadn't called out his name or even moved from her seat.

She'd watched in horror as he'd walked away from her and out of the shop. In an instant all her fears had been confirmed. She had no longer been able to deny that he knew she was in New York and he'd wanted nothing to do with her.

She looked up to see that Chloe wasn't eating. She glanced at her own plate, which was almost full with her favorite pesto linguine that she had no appetite for. "Do you want to get this to go?"

"Yes, please. I'm exhausted," Chloe replied. As they waited for the check it was Chloe who broke the comfortable silence.

"Kate, can you think of any reason why Matt walked away from you?"

"I've thought of every reason. The only one that justifies his actions is that he really didn't love me."

"You're sure?"

"Yes."

"So what do you want now?"

"I want the impossible. I want to trust the man I love to love me back and not break my heart again."

CHAPTER NINE

IT WAS ANOTHER week before she heard from Matt again. A whole week to replay their entire relationship from their friendship to the night they'd made love, and the repercussions that had followed.

Kate was once again in the emergency department, reviewing consultations with the junior residents, when her pager went off. She looked down at the little black box that seemed forever attached to her and didn't recognize the number.

She reached for the nearest phone and dialed the displayed number. "This is Kate Spence. Someone paged?" she answered once the person on the other end picked up.

"It's Matt."

She paused, not sure what to say. Her conversation with Chloe had helped her understand her feelings towards Matt and it felt even harder to talk to him knowing she still loved him.

"Kate." Matt said her name.

"I'm here." She had lowered her voice, not sure where the conversation was headed but knowing she didn't want it overheard.

"We need to get together to talk about that night," Matt stated, in what Kate considered to be an overly businesslike tone for something so intimate, something so personal. She arched her back in defense and looked around the crowded emergency department to ensure that no one was within earshot.

"I gave you more than enough opportunity to talk about that night nine years ago, Matt. I don't want to talk about it now." She waited and heard him exhale slowly.

"I meant the night that Mr. Weber died, Kate. I need to finish your statement to help with the case. But, for the record, a talk about the other night is long overdue."

It was her turn to sigh now. She felt embarrassed and could feel color flooding her face. She looked down and studied the linoleum floor as if the more intensely she stared, the more she could avoid Matt's presence on the other end of the phone.

"I can meet you after you're done working," Matt offered, saving her from having to respond to his earlier statement.

"Okay, but not at the hospital." She actually didn't know where the best place to talk with Matt was. Nowhere, she thought. She wanted to avoid a public scene but it would be worse to be together in a private place.

"I'll pick you up at nine—will that give you enough time to finish up? You can tell me then where you want to go." He was giving her control, but the gesture did little to put her at ease.

"Yes, that's fine. I'll be waiting outside my place at nine. See you then." And she hung up before she could embarrass herself further.

Matt was becoming more of a contradiction each time she talked to him. Everything she had believed about him was changing. She'd thought he didn't want her, but now he did. She'd thought what they had been together had been a lie, but he'd said she'd belong to him always. Now, after nine years, he thought they needed to talk about that night, after he had done everything possible to avoid doing that.

Kate returned to the waiting resident and did her best to focus on the patient's history. After examining the middle-aged woman together and then arranging her admission for management of a partial small bowel obstruction, it was eight p.m., and Kate found herself sprinting home.

By the time she entered the brownstone apartment she was breathless. She had twenty minutes before Matt would be arriving, and she knew she had just enough time to shower and change. Years of rushing to and from the hospital at a moment's notice had taught her to be efficient.

She showered and washed her hair, toweling it dry and twisting it into a knot on top of her head. She rubbed in the lotion her skin desperately needed after long days spent in the dry, non-infectious conditions the hospital maintained. In her bedroom, she managed to find a pair of clean jeans and a long-sleeved black sweater. She was just bending to put on socks when the front buzzer rang. She slipped her feet into tall black leather boots, grabbed her wool coat and applied lip moisturizer as she locked her apartment and proceeded down the stairs to meet Matt.

He was waiting in the entry. He had obviously been home since the office, because the business suit was gone and in its place was a pair of dark jeans with a dress shirt and blue sweater layered over the top. Despite the layered look there was no mistaking the broadness of his shoulders and the build of his chest. The chest she had seen, had felt pressed against her. Damn, this is not what she needed to be thinking.

Matt didn't say anything. He held open the front door to her building and followed her out to his car, where he opened the passenger door for her as well. Once she was settled he closed the door securely and circled to the driver's side. It felt like being taken care of, it felt nice, and she didn't want to be feeling that again with Matt.

"Where do you want to go?" Matt asked, turning towards her with his full attention.

"I don't know," Kate answered honestly, too off balance by the situation to think properly.

"We should probably go somewhere private where our discussion can't be overheard if we're talking about the case. That leaves out public restaurants. So the options are my office or my apartment—"

"Office," Kate answered, before Matt had even finished. There was no way she wanted to be back in his apartment with him. Things had gotten way out of control the other night and she would be a fool to think that couldn't happen again.

"Okay, as you wish." He shifted the car into gear and they entered traffic. Kate avoided small talk, not knowing what to say, what it was safe to say, in this new weird dynamic between them. They wove down the streets of Boston towards Matt's office.

They arrived and Matt parked in the underground garage. He used a swipe card to open the door and unlock the elevator that carried them up to his top-floor office. Once inside, he led her through, not to his office, where she would actually have been uncomfortable given their last interaction there, but to a conference room.

The view was beautiful. Floor-to-ceiling glass windows highlighted Boston at night. The sight of the whole city spread out in front of her made her feel less important and actually calmer about the impending discussion.

"Sparkling water okay for you?" Matt asked, breaking her attention from the beauty of the city.

"Sure." She took her place in one of the chairs opposite him. "Where do you want to start?" she asked.

He nodded at her and took out a pen and pad of paper. "What was your official role the evening of Mr. Weber's death?"

"I was the chief surgical resident. I serve as backup in all situations—resident illness, difficult cases and high patient volumes. That night the on-call resident, Dr. Jensen, had been called away to do a retrieval with the transplant team, and I was called in in his absence." Okay, so maybe this was going to be okay, clean, surgical. She relaxed back into the leather conference room chair.

"What was Dr. Reed's official role?"

"Dr. Reed was the second on-call vascular surgeon. We have a backup system for all the major surgical disciplines so that in the event a surgeon is tied up in a prolonged surgical case, another patient can still receive timely care and surgical management."

"How often is the second on call needed?"

"About once every three months, but Tate might be better able to answer that question."

"Dr. Reed," Matt stated firmly.

"Pardon?" Kate asked, not understanding what the question was.

"Refer to Tate Reed as Dr. Reed in all your discussion of the case. Referring to him as Tate implies you know him beyond your professional relationship."

Kate couldn't tell if this was just Matt the lawyer

talking or if it was personal. She decided she didn't need to know and waited from him to ask another question.

"When were you asked to consult in Mr. Weber's care?"

"At about ten p.m. I was already in-house, dealing with some issues in a postoperative patient, when the emergency room doctor called me."

"How soon after did you see him?"

"I went downstairs to the emergency department immediately and started my assessment. While I was examining him, the radiologist called and notified me of the CT scan findings."

"When did you first try to contact Dr. Reed?" Matt lowered and softened his voice for this question. They were getting into the part of the evening that was less clinical and more personal.

"I called Dr. Reed on his cell phone immediately after I finished on the phone with the radiologist."

"How many times did you try to call Dr. Reed?"

"I didn't count, I just kept redialing when I didn't get through."

"Did you leave any messages?"

"Yes."

"Was it unusual for Dr. Reed not to answer his cellphone?"

"Yes." She wasn't elaborating on her responses or providing any additional information. The lawyer in Matt actually seemed pleased about that.

"Were there any other occasions when Dr. Reed did not answer his phone?"

"Not prior to that night."

"Did you have any reason to believe that Dr. Reed was purposely ignoring his calls?"

Here it goes, time to get personal. She took a deep

breath and straightened away from the chair, sitting upright and focusing her eyes directly on Matt's.

"After trying to contact Dr. Reed for twenty minutes,
I concluded that he was probably unaware that the attempts being made to contact him were for patient care
and subsequently asked the switchboard to reach him."

"Was his primary contact number for patient care
his cell phone?"

"Yes."

"Then why would he not answer it in his role as second call?"

"That is a question for Dr. Reed. I cannot speak to
why he would or would not do something."

"You were always too smart for your own good,
Kate." He reached down and pulled his sweater off,
leaving the dress shirt behind. Then he unbuttoned the
cuffs and rolled the sleeves up, exposing his muscled
forearms. He leaned on them and stared at her across
the table. "I have a copy of Dr. Reed's phone records
from that night, as does the plaintiff's attorney. They
show several calls from your cell phone to Dr. Reed's,
all lasting less than a minute."

"As I stated, I tried to call Dr. Reed for twenty
minutes before relinquishing the responsibility to the
switchboard."

"The calls from you start at eight-thirty p.m., well
before your interaction with Mr. Weber."

"Yes." She wasn't going to give more detail. She had
no intention of describing to Matt, Tate's proposal and
the reasons behind her rejection.

"If Dr. Reed had not answered your earlier calls, do
you think it was appropriate to spend twenty minutes
using the same form of contact that had been ineffec-

tive up until that point?" He wasn't enjoying this, she could tell, and that was at least something.

"I was using the form of communication listed by the hospital as Dr. Reed's first contact. When that failed I appropriately moved on to the switchboard as second contact and focused on Mr. Weber, pending Dr. Reed's contact and arrival."

"Your attempts to contact Dr. Reed earlier in the evening, were they related to patient care?"

"No."

"You have a personal relationship with Dr. Reed?" It was more of a statement than a question. She knew where this was going.

"Yes."

"What is your relationship with Dr. Reed?" He was agitated now. He ran his fingers through his hair. It was going to be a mutually uncomfortable conversation.

"We have worked together for several years and are friends." Honest, she was being honest.

"Do you have a romantic relationship with Dr. Reed?"

"No."

"What was your relationship with Dr. Reed the night of Mr. Weber's death?"

"I was the chief resident and Dr. Reed was the staff surgeon."

"What was the nature of your personal relationship with Dr. Reed the night of Mr. Weber's death?" Matt asked pointedly, his entire attention fixed on Kate.

"We had been dating for one and a half years."

"Was there anything about your personal relationship that night that would have led Dr. Reed to not answer your calls?"

"Once again that is a question for Dr. Reed. I cannot speak to why he would or would not do something."

"Did you and Dr. Reed end your romantic involvement that night?" His jaw was clenched and she could see the muscle tense as it extended towards his temple. She hadn't seen Matt angry a lot when they had first known one another, but she recognized it now.

"Yes."

"Kate," he sighed, and ran his fingers through his hair again, "you are answering like you are talking to the enemy, which I'm not. If this ever gets to court then, yes, this is the exact way you are to testify, but tonight, with me, you need to open up. I need to know what happened if I'm going to help you."

"Are you sure that's the only reason you want to know?" It was direct and she didn't back down with her question or when she held his eyes. What she'd had with Matt in the past had been a lie and she damn sure wasn't going to continue to let anything but the truth be between them now. He didn't answer.

"It's not the only reason." She looked up as he started his response and saw heat in his eyes. They were locked on hers and she felt her whole body flush and pulse in response. What had seemed like a good idea, to call Matt out, now seemed an obvious, horrible mistake. The detached tone of their earlier conversation had left and everything personal was flooding in. She didn't know how to respond, couldn't respond, as her lips parted and she struggled to breathe in and out.

"Kate, are you sure you're ready to hear more? Are you ready to ask me about the things you want to know?" He was being gentle in his voice, the same soft whisper that had once been in her ear, the same careful handling when she was clearly in over her head.

"Why now, Matt? What's changed?"

"Everything, and nothing, Kate. I'm not the same man you knew, just as you aren't the same woman, but what's between us hasn't gone away and never will." He reached out and covered her hand with his. It felt warm, and strong, and all-encompassing.

"There wasn't anything between us." She pulled her hand from under his and tucked both hands under her legs, away from the temptation to touch him. She couldn't let herself get drawn back into the belief that their love was mutual.

"How can you say that, Kate? How can you speak to how I felt about us?" He was lawyering her now, using her own argument about not speaking for someone else against her. It left her cold and brought out the clear, precise, objective words and voice she used as a surgeon.

"Because you told me. You looked me in the eye the morning after we made love and you said, 'Katie, I'm sorry. I don't love you.' Then you proved it by walking out and not coming back, not answering my calls, my e-mails, my letters, and running from the sight of me. That's how I know how you felt about us." The ache in her throat was intensifying but she was not going to cry, despite the burning feeling that was pooling behind her eyes.

"I lied to you."

Her eyes flew to his.

"Why? Why would you do that? Was I that disappointing? That bad in bed that it was worth throwing everything else that was good about us away?" Gone now was her composure and with it her pride, and out came the most painful thought she had buried deep within her and avoided voicing at all costs.

She placed her elbows on her legs and buried her face

in her hands, unable to face him any longer, unable to hear his response and horrified that she had asked the question. Within seconds she was being lifted from her seat. Matt had reached for her beneath her arms and raised her out of her chair. Startled, she wrapped her arms around his neck for balance and he wrapped his arms around her further, gathering her to him.

Then he crushed his mouth to hers. It wasn't soft, it wasn't gentle, it was possessive. The pressure of his lips parted hers and he began to taste her and explore her mouth as if he was a dying man searching for his last drink of water. She was angry, surprised, and entranced all at the same time, until the same urgency and passion from the other night took hold.

She ran her tongue across his lower lip, her response escalating the passion between them. At some point he walked them up against a wall and pressed her against it, shifting her to place himself between her legs and holding her by her bottom, his hands firm and solid. Warmth was spreading through her body until she felt like she was on fire. When they finally broke apart, both were gasping and he slowly slid her down his length to the floor, his erection prominent in the journey.

He cupped one side of her face and brought her gaze to his, and it was the same old Matt. He put his finger against her lips and silenced her before she could talk. "You are the most perfect woman I have ever met, both in bed and out. No woman before or after has ever compared to you. Not a day has gone by in the last nine years that I haven't wanted to be with you, to hold you, to kiss every inch of your naked body and move inside you until you scream out my name over and over and over again."

"No." She shook her head against his words, looking away from the man who was confusing her mind and body.

"Yes, Kate," he said as he cupped the side of her face again, bringing her eyes to his.

"I don't believe you," she said. Actions were more important than words, and his actions had spoken so loudly.

"I did it for you, Kate, I walked away for you, not for me. You were going to throw away medical school, everything you had worked for. You were the most perfect, selfless woman I had ever met and I wasn't going allow anything to change you or take away your dreams."

She was stunned by his claim, both by the audacity of the lie and how truthful and heartfelt he seemed to be while making it. She took a deep breath and very clearly and slowly spoke to Matt, looking him in the eye and searching for the truth. "So what you are saying is that if I had been strong enough and gone to medical school in New York, you wouldn't have broken my heart and walked out on me without looking back?"

"If you had been in New York, I wouldn't have been strong enough to stay away from you, even if I thought it was for your own good." The passionate statement fueled her own passion and she reached out and slapped him across his cheek. The sound echoed across the conference room and she was shocked silent by her own action, drawing her hand up to touch her own cheek, mirroring his reaction. She was horrified by her response yet unwilling to apologize.

"It's been nine years, Matt, you don't need to bother lying to me any more."

She didn't let him reply. He seemed shocked by the turn of events in the last few minutes. She grabbed her jacket and purse and left the conference room, searching for the quickest way out. She didn't have a keycard to access anything, so instead she headed for the fire stairwell and fled down the twenty-five flights into the building alley. Her heart was pounding as the sound of her boots echoed on the cement stairs. In the dark, in the cold, she caught her breath, her chest heaving. He wanted her. He wanted her enough to lie to her to get her back.

CHAPTER TEN

SHE WAS FROZEN. The wind was blowing strongly off the harbor and the wet coldness was seeping through every inch of her body. She walked quickly through the cobblestoned old roads of Boston that wound their way through the city's core from Matt's office back to her apartment. Why had Matt lied to her? What purpose did it serve? Nothing made sense, and she couldn't tell what hurt more, Matt's lies or that for a moment she had believed him.

It had taken so long to learn how to trust herself again, but she had, and a lot of that feeling had come from her confidence and success in medicine. She had even felt happy and contented with her life, leaving the past and Matt behind, until Tate had proposed.

Tate on one knee in front of her with a ring, and she had seen Matt. Pain didn't begin to describe the way she had felt when she'd realized she wasn't in love with the man in front of her, and that deep inside Matt was still trapped in her heart.

When were those feeling going to go away? Matt wasn't the same man she had known back at Brown, but that didn't seem to make a difference. The way she sensed him when he walked in a room hadn't changed. The way she felt when he touched her had changed, but unfortunately had increased a thousand times over in the intensity she felt go through her the moment his lips or hands touched her body. It was the only time her mind forgot about everything that had happened between them.

Thoughts of the passion tempered the cold she was feeling and she quickened her pace. She could have hailed a cab, but the clear, cold night air was a needed contrast to the storm she was feeling inside. Forty-five minutes later she reached the steps of her apartment, not failing to notice the large expensive sports car and the man behind the wheel a few doors down. So it was not over for tonight, she thought to herself.

She let herself into her apartment and turned on the kettle. What she really wanted was a glass of bourbon, something to warm her through, but she would have to settle for tea, begrudging the responsibility of the pager she carried. She brought her cup to the couch, curled into the charcoal-gray throw blanket and waited. It was ten minutes before the buzzer sounded and she walked to the intercom, buzzed him in and propped open the door. She resigned herself to another conversation that would hurt and bring her no answers or closure.

He walked through the door without words. She watched him expectantly as he closed and locked the door, took off his jacket and made his way towards the couch. He still didn't say anything as he picked up her legs, which had been running across the cushions lengthwise, and redeposited them on his lap, taking the time to wrap her feet in the blanket-ends to make sure they didn't get cold.

"We don't have anything more to say to each other," she finally said.

"We have a lot more to say to each other and you

know it, Kate. The problem is that you don't believe what I'm saying." He was subconsciously stroking the sole of her foot with his thumb but didn't look at her.

"What's in this for you, Matt? I don't understand what you want. Why are you saying and doing all these things?"

"I want you," he said simply, finally turning to look at her, his gaze unwavering.

"Now," she stated flatly as she pulled her knees to her chest, and her feet and legs away from his touch. "You want me now," she said. "What has changed your mind? It is Tate?"

If jealousy was what was fueling this, then she was going to call him on it. There would be no more lies or words left unsaid between them. She watched as he reacted to her words: his jaw tightened and his fingers clenched into his palms. He stayed like that for what seemed like an eternity but must have only been a few seconds.

"Tate Reed is a good man, but you don't belong with him, Kate, you belong with me, you always have."

"No, Matt, I don't. Our past together has proved that. We had our chance together and it wasn't enough for you, and this change of heart isn't enough for me." She hadn't even known herself that was how she felt until the words were out of her mouth. She looked at him and understood that part of him was right, she would always be his, but she couldn't trust him, and without trust they couldn't move forward.

"Kate, when was the last time you trusted me?" He knew her too well. He also probably knew the honest response. That night when he'd asked her if she trusted him and then made love to her. She was going to be honest, even if he wasn't.

"Our last night together at Brown."

"When was the last time you believed I loved you?"

"The same."

He didn't say anything. He reached over and lifted her towards him as though she weighed nothing. He placed her astride him, and she had to place her hands on his shoulders to stop herself from colliding with him. He gently pushed her hair away from her face and pressed his lips to hers. It was them, as they had been.

His lips were soft, the only soft part of a hard man. He didn't make any move to deepen this kiss, to open her to him. She felt him pull away and opened her eyes with surprise. He had tangled his hand in her hair and from her position on his hips she could feel the hard bulge pressing into the core of her. But he wasn't moving any further and treacherously she wanted him to.

"Kate…" He quickly touched his lips to hers again before continuing. "Let me prove to you that I love you." He swept her hair away from her neck and started pressing his lips against its length.

Did he love her? She didn't know, just as she didn't know if she could ever trust him enough to believe the words she had waited so long to hear.

"What if you can't?" she whispered, her sense of reason managing to escape before it was completely lost to his touch.

He stopped and cupped the side of her face, returning his eyes to hers. "I will, Kate. This desire, this passion between us is there for a reason, and it's not going away. I'm not going away."

Of all the words he could have said, the promise not to leave was the most important thing for her to hear.

He wanted her. She believed that from his touch and the physical pull between them. He'd said he'd lied, but when? Had it been nine years ago or tonight? Did it matter? The only truth she knew was that she wanted him too and that feeling was not going away. Risks versus benefit, she thought to herself. She was pretty sure he couldn't break her the way she had been broken before, but maybe being with him again would help heal the wounds that had been left between them. Or maybe it would simply cure her burning need to experience again what had been physically and emotionally so nearly perfect that night all those years ago.

She moved her hands from his shoulders and ran her fingers through his hair as she returned her lips to his. She tugged gently at his lower lip, a physical act of agreement, and he responded. The pressure from his lips increased and she felt her lips part as his tongue swept their thin line. She opened her mouth to him and savored the feeling of him exploring and tasting her, responding with equal fervor. He broke from her mouth and moved along her neck as his hands swept under her shirt along her bare back.

Moving forward, his thumbs brushed the sides of her breasts, and her need increased a hundred times over. She reached down to the hem of her shirt, pulling it over her head and off her overheated body. Then she did the same to Matt, wanting to feel their bare skin touching. He kissed her again as their bodies pressed and she instinctively ground her throbbing core against him.

She sighed with relief when she felt the clasp of her bra unhook and the weight of her now heavy breasts drop. She pulled away slightly and Matt threaded the black lace bra off her body. She experienced satisfaction, watching and feeling him cup her breasts in his hands. His thumbs traced the outline of her nipples before rolling them gently between his fingers. It was torture, sweet, sweet torture. She moaned the word "More" and watched Matt smile a very familiar smile as he took the nipple into his mouth. His other hand never left the other breast and it was hard to cope with all the different sensations of pleasure running through her body. She needed something to focus on or she thought she might actually faint from the intensity of his touch.

She ran her hands down the hard, flat plane of his abdomen to the waistband of his jeans. She tugged open the belt, button and zipper, releasing him into her hand. He was so hard that he easily slipped through the fly opening in his underwear, allowing her to touch and caress his naked length. Her hand stroked his entire length, fantasizing about the moment when all of him would be inside her. Her thumb circled his tip, slick already with desire. She felt his hold on her breast and the intensity with which he was sucking her nipple increase as he groaned against her.

"Kate," he moaned, as he released her breasts so that he could use his hands to gently remove hers from him. Gray eyes met blue as they stared at each other with looks of agreement about where this was headed.

She pulled herself up off his lap and led him down the hall towards her bedroom. She didn't turn on a light but the uncovered window allowed in the city's nightlight glow, which reflected off their bodies. She finished what she had started and while standing in front of Matt, facing him, she removed the rest of her clothing. He stepped towards her and she removed his as well, until they were both naked.

His hands returned to her face and hair and he pressed his lips against hers again, like the calm before the storm. Kate gasped as he lifted her from her feet and deposited her on the bed. She felt a shiver course through her body and couldn't tell if it was from the night air against her naked skin or from anticipation.

She didn't stay cold for long. She watched Matt study her before he joined her, covering her body with his own. She savored the feel of the weight and the heat of him against her. She opened her hips as each leg wrapped around him until he was positioned perfectly, as much her doing as his.

He didn't enter her. He stayed motionless below the waist, even though she was arching and pushing against him. He started kissing her again, her lips, her neck, her breasts and nipples. His body weight was held on one arm and as Kate writhed beneath him she unconsciously absorbed the beautiful architecture of the muscles in that arm and shoulder. His free hand caressed down her side towards the inside of her thigh. She had never wanted something so badly and she grabbed his hips in an attempt to pull him forward, but again he resisted.

She felt his lips and the stubble of his cheek return to her neck when he again moaned against her. "Kate, I'm trying really hard to take things slow this time and make love to you the way I should have, but you're making it really, really hard."

"Please, Matt," she begged, still struggling towards his final possession. She could see the change in him. His resolution faded and the small upward turn of a smile appeared at the corner of his mouth.

He stroked her leg one last time from her bottom to the knee that was crooked around his back. His hands went to either side of her head as he pressed forward and she felt the tip of him at her entrance. The slight touch after the agony of waiting caused her to catch her breath and close her eyes with pleasure.

"Kate, open your eyes and look at me."

She did so and the moment they made contact he pushed into her so deeply that she didn't know where he ended and she began. He moved slowly at first, his eyes never leaving hers as he stroked within her. There was no pain this time, just pleasure and a sense of completeness that she didn't want to examine. With every touch of him she couldn't imagine being able to stand the exquisiteness of another touch, and then he pushed in again. She could feel her body working with his as her muscles tightened against him, and he responded by moving more deeply inside. She felt panicky as the surges of pleasure started to build and she couldn't stop them, couldn't stop the release that was coming so quickly. She teetered on the edge, trying to hold on, trying to prolong the intimacy and connection between them.

"Kate, trust me, let go." His words, accompanied by almost complete withdrawal and a deep thrust, sealed her fate as she finally broke eye contact, closing her eyes and arching her back as she climaxed and tears of release streamed down her face. Her first aftershock was almost as powerful as her orgasm and was joined by a growl from Matt as he buried his head against her and cried out as she felt him spill into her.

She struggled to catch her breath, but equally calmly savored the weight of him collapsed against her. His lips brushed against her cheek, tasting the saltiness of her tears. She wasn't sure how long they remained that way, contented and too spent to move.

The shrill of her pager startled them both. Matt pulled out and away from her and she felt instantly bereft. The second beep focused her attention on the little black box that was still clipped to her jeans, lying discarded on the bedroom floor. She moved off the bed and unclipped the device, pushing the solitary button and registering the number of the emergency department.

"I'm sorry," she murmured. She found the portable phone and dialed the number, her back turned towards Matt.

"It's Dr. Spence. I was paged to this number."

"It's Ryan Callum." Dr. Callum was one of the senior emergency attending physicians, and if her alarm hadn't been raised before, it was now.

"Kate, I'm calling about Chloe Darcy. During her shift tonight she was found unconscious in the doctors' change room." Any self-conscious feeling she had about standing naked answering a page faded in place of fear as her heart started pounding in her chest and the blood seemed to drain from her body.

"Oh, my God." She slumped down onto the edge of the bed. "Where is Chloe now?" It was hard to contain her panic. This wasn't a patient, this was her best friend.

"She's in Section A of the emergency department. Kate, I'm calling because you are listed as her emergency contact on her health forms."

"I'll be right there." Section A was not good. If Chloe had just fainted from exhaustion or low blood sugar she would be in a lower acuity part of the department. Section A was reserved for critical patients requiring continuous monitoring and one-on-one care.

She stood, turned and collided with Matt, her naked body flattening against him. He had pulled on his underwear and jeans, but his shirt was still in the living room. His arms reached around to steady her and then quickly released her. He handed her a robe, which she batted away, and then he left the bedroom as she searched for new clothing. In less than thirty seconds she was ready and in the living room, where Matt stood holding the front door of the apartment open.

"I'm driving you." It was not a request, it was a statement, and she found herself grateful for his decisiveness as she was feeling more panicky than she could ever remember feeling.

She was gripped with fear as Matt sped towards the hospital. She couldn't talk, her thoughts stuck on repeat in her head. Chloe was her best friend, her rock. Chloe had gotten her through Matt's abandonment. Chloe had supported her through the breakup with Tate. But where had she herself been when Chloe had needed her? She had been self-destructing with Matt. Guilt coursed through her, thinking of the pleasure she had been experiencing while Chloe had been lying unconscious, waiting to be found.

Her friend had not been herself the other day. Kate had noticed that she had looked tired and pale, but Chloe had reassured her that it was just a virus. Kate had been so wrapped up in her own problems she hadn't taken the time Chloe had needed, like a good friend, like a good doctor, should have. Her mind raced as she established the differential diagnosis for viral illness and syncope. For a healthy woman to be in a critical condition it either had to involve her cardiac, respiratory or neurological systems, or a combination of them. If it was her heart, that would mean myocarditis and inflammation of the heart, leading to abnormal rhythms or, worse, a cardiomyopathy or valve damage, leading to permanent disability. If it was respiratory, then it would be an aggressive coronavirus like the SARS outbreak a few years back that had led to the deaths of many health care workers. If it was neurological, then it would be meningitis, which could lead to permanent neurological impairment.

"Stop." Matt's voice broke through her thoughts. She turned and looked at him, though his eyes didn't leave the road. "She's going to be okay."

"You can't know that," Kate replied in a scared whisper. She wanted in her heart to believe what Matt was saying, but rationally she knew that there was no way to predict sometimes what would happen. She had been in medicine long enough to understand that bad things happened to good people for no reason at all, and Chloe was the best person she knew.

Before they could talk more, Matt pulled into the emergency room loading dock. She took one glance at him, and heard him tell her to go as she jumped out of the car. She raced through the automatic doors and through the emergency department to Section A. She reached the large, wall-mounted computer screen that tracked patients, searching for Chloe's identifier. She saw 30F listed under room four, thirty-year-old female—that would be Chloe. She controlled the desire to keeping running, and walked quickly to room four.

She wasn't prepared for the sight that greeted her. The room was empty but not cleaned. Her eyes darted around as her mind pieced together the information her eyes were processing. The stretcher was gone, so that meant that Chloe was somewhere in the hospital, having been transported on said stretcher. The floor was smeared with blood, not a lot of blood but enough. The rapid transfuser was in the room, a sign that Chloe had required a blood transfusion. In the sink she saw several empty IV bags, more evidence of vascular collapse. The scene before her was compatible with only two scenarios. One was a severe viral infection, leading to hemolytic anemia and septic shock. The other was hypovolemic shock secondary to acute blood loss. Either way, Chloe was very, very sick.

She left the room and her eyes searched the unit for Ryan Callum, but she couldn't see him. When she didn't immediately see anyone who would be useful in helping her locate Chloe, she left the department with a list of three possible locations in mind. Radiology, Intensive Care Unit, or the operating room. Chloe had to be in one of those locations.

She went to the main floor radiology unit first. The one benefit of doing nothing but work for the past four and a half years was that everyone in the hospital recognized her, even out of scrubs, and was quick to provide her with the information she wanted. Chloe wasn't in Radiology, neither was she in the intensive care unit. That left the operating room and Kate's fear increased. She went to the OR change room, put on scrubs and covered her hair to allow herself access to all areas.

It was after hours, which meant that only a few of the operating theatres were still running. She walked the hall, looking for activity and lights. She stopped dead in her tracks when she saw Tate staring through the small rectangular window of an operating-room door.

He didn't notice her. He just stared, transfixed, through the window.

"Tate," she said quietly, as she placed a hand on his shoulder.

He didn't turn to look at her, keeping his eyes glued on the window. "I think she's stabilizing. They kicked me out of the room, so I can't tell for sure. But they have stopped calling for blood and I can see the anesthesia monitors and her heart rate has come down to the one-twenties and her blood pressure is back up."

"What happened?" Kate asked, desperately wanting to see for herself.

"I don't know, they won't tell me anything. The usual patient confidentiality, etc. I only got here about fifteen minutes ago. I was checking the operating-room board to see how many cases were lined up for tonight at the front desk when the porter from the blood bank came to drop off blood. I overheard him verifying Chloe's name and blood-bank number with the unit clerk."

"Who is in with her?"

"Gynecology," he said, his resentment coming through clearly.

"Oh." Kate felt some understanding drift in. The department of obstetrics and gynecology was a separate surgical department from the department of general surgery. While both groups worked in the same operating rooms, the two disciplines kept to themselves with little understanding of the ins and outs of each other's fields.

"Is it a hemorrhagic ovarian cyst?" Kate asked, still needing answers.

"I don't know, Kate. Like I said, they won't tell me anything." She stopped asking questions.

It was right that they were guarding Chloe's privacy, but at the same time it was intensely aggravating. Being in the health care field, she had become used to having access to people's confidential information. Only this time she and Tate were not responsible for Chloe's care, so they had no need to have access to that information other than for their personal interest, which did not entitle them to it.

She and Tate stood there for another twenty minutes before Kate had had enough. Let them throw her out, let them reprimand her even for her inappropriate behavior. She was already being sued. This, at least, would be worth the consequences.

Without words, she gently pushed Tate to the side and went through the operating-room door. She wasn't ready for what she saw, despite it being an everyday scene. It felt completely different when the person on the operating table was someone you loved. Chloe was lying there, surrounded by the surgical team. There were two anesthetists at the head of the table, two scrub nurses, and what looked like three people from the gynecology team. She looked at the faces and recognized Erin Madden, the chief gynecology resident, whom she had met on several occasions over their years in training.

"Hi, Kate." Erin acknowledged her presence, though her eyes didn't deviate from Chloe's abdomen, which was open on the operating room table.

Part of Kate wanted to get closer, but she wasn't sure she was ready emotionally to see Chloe so exposed. She also didn't want to push her luck and risk getting thrown out, as Tate had.

"She's going to be okay. We have evacuated the hemoperitoneum and have stopped the bleeding. We are going to be closing in the next few minutes and then she will be going to Recovery, followed by a short stay in the intensive care unit in case she runs into any massive transfusion complications."

"Uh-huh." Kate nodded, trying to process the information she was being given.

"I'm sorry we had to open her, Kate. We tried with the laprascope but she had too much blood in her abdomen and was too unstable to tolerate it."

"But the bleeding has been stopped?" Kate asked, unable to keep herself from surveying the room, her eyes focused on the evidence of what looked like a massive blood loss.

"Yes."

"What happened?" Kate finally asked.

"That's not for me to disclose to you, Kate. Chloe will be able to tell you herself later, if she chooses to. I think you should go now and take Dr. Reed with you. She is stable and we'll take good care of her. You can see her in the intensive care unit in a couple of hours, once she's settled in."

"Okay," Kate said, resigned, knowing she would get no more from Erin. "Thank you," she said to the team that had obviously saved Chloe's life.

She left the room, gently pushing on the door to make sure it didn't hit Tate. He hadn't moved.

"She's okay. They won't tell me what happened, but they opened her, stopped whatever was bleeding, and she's stabilized. She's going to go to the intensive care unit for a short while because of the large amount of blood products she received."

"Thank you, Kate," Tate replied. His eyes were still trained on the window and he didn't budge from his spot outside the door.

"Tate, they have asked us to leave the operating room and I think we should. She's stable and there is nothing we can do for her except get in the way and distract the team."

"I'm not leaving her."

"We're not leaving her, Tate. We are helping her by getting out of the way and letting them do their jobs. The same thing we ask other people to do for us." She grabbed his arm and pulled him a little to ease him away from his spot.

"Tate, we need to go. You know Chloe would never

want us to see her like this." It was true, but she still felt mean, using guilt to move Tate away.

"Are you in love with Matt McKayne?" he asked, with no reproach or anger left in his voice.

She was shocked both by the abrupt change in the conversation and the directness of the question itself. So much so that she answered without thinking about her response. "Yes, I think I always have been, even when I hated him."

"Then you should be with him. Forget everything that has gone wrong between you and be together."

"It's not that simple, Tate. I can't trust him."

"Kate, that's not simple," he replied, pointing towards the door. Then he took one last look through the window and walked away from both Chloe and Kate.

CHAPTER ELEVEN

AFTER DROPPING KATE off at the emergency entrance doors, Matt waited. The admitting office had informed him that Dr. Darcy would be going to the intensive care unit and Matt found his way to the unit's family waiting room and waited. In the three hours he waited for Kate he replayed all the scenes of the past, including the one tonight.

She had known it was him. For the first time there was not a single doubt in his mind about whom Kate wanted. She had used his name and kept her eyes open as they had made love and it had been the most powerful sexual experience he had ever had. She really was the most perfect and beautiful woman he had ever met.

The hard waiting-room chair he sat on and the coffee-machine brew he sipped were a stark contrast to the earlier events of the evening. He cringed both at the coffee and at his unfair resentment and anger towards her pager and her job. It was irrational to feel resentful when Chloe Darcy was fighting for her life, but he still had the feeling. He had finally been getting through to Kate. Physically they were on the same page and he was angry that they were not going to have the rest of the night to work towards resolving the remaining distance between them. There was still some part of the picture he was missing, something that was holding Kate back from opening up to him completely.

Ever since he had returned he had assumed that something had been Tate. The pair's past relationship, that first night together when they had almost made love and she had stopped suddenly, the night he'd seen them together at her apartment, and the obvious continued connection and trust between them had left him with little other explanation. But he had been wrong. He was certain now that they were not together romantically. Kate was Kate and she would never have made love with him if she was in love and involved with another man, he was certain of that. So what explanation did he have for her refusal to believe the truth and her violent reaction towards him and his long-ago reasoning?

He shifted uncomfortably in his seat, having to purposefully steer his mind from the graphic images from earlier tonight that were etched in his mind. The site of Kate and Tate walking through the intensive care unit's automatic doors helped his cause.

He studied them, looking for signs of how Chloe was and also in an attempt to define their relationship. There was a familiarity, a trust between them that he envied.

Kate had changed into her hospital scrubs, the dark blue matching the smudges under her eyes.

"How is she?" he asked. Tate took a moment to look at Kate, though Matt had no idea what meaning was meant to be expressed.

"Excuse me," Tate said, before he walked away down the hall of the busy unit.

"She's going to be okay." Kate's voice brought his attention back to her.

"What happened to her?" He knew enough about medicine from his work in medical defense to know that healthy young women did not end up in the intensive care unit without a serious reason.

"We don't know. Well, the doctors who worked on her know, but they are maintaining her right to confidentiality," she replied, her frustration and despair obvious. She pulled the elastic band from her hair, allowing it to tumble around her shoulders in an effort to release tension. He reached out and drew her to him, wrapping his arms around her, and was comforted when she relaxed into him. He didn't say anything, didn't want to break this of respite between them. He moved his hand up to the base of her head and gently massaged the tense muscles beneath his fingers.

He didn't know how long they stood together, but he savored every second. She finally pulled away and stepped back to look at him. "I need to check on Chloe, shower, and get to work."

He placed his hands on her upper arms, not wanting to break their connection. "What can I do, Kate?"

"Nothing, there is nothing you can do. I have a change of clothes and toiletries here so I don't need to go home. Tate is on nights this week, so between us one of us can always be with Chloe. I need to focus on her, Matt. She needs to be my priority." There was a clear message in her statement, and Matt knew better than to try to change her mind. Kate would spend twenty-four hours a day at the hospital if that was what it took to do her job and be with Chloe. She had ranked her priorities, Chloe and then work. He wasn't on her list, despite what had happened between them.

"Promise me you'll call me if you need something, Kate. I would also like to know how Chloe does. She seems like a good person."

"Yeah, she really is." She sighed and then drew a

deep breath and squared her shoulders. "I need to go. Thank you for being here." Then she broke free and walked away.

Matt left the hospital just as the sun was rising in the cold spring air. He stopped at his apartment to shower and change clothes and was in the office by seven. He knew that there was nothing he could do to help with Chloe's recovery, but he could do the one thing he had been hired to do, and get Kate out of the lawsuit.

He had reviewed the file and after talking to Tate and Kate he had a clear understanding of the events of that evening. Tate and Kate had been together, and that night Tate had ended their relationship. Kate had been upset and had made several attempts to talk to Tate and he had ignored her calls to his cell phone. Kate had then been called back into the hospital, where she had been when she'd been consulted on Mr. Weber's care. After the results of the CT scan had established the diagnosis, Kate had organized Mr. Weber's care and made attempts to contact Tate Reed as the second on-call vascular surgeon. She had reached him via the switchboard within twenty minutes and Mr. Weber had been in the operating theatre within twenty minutes of that contact. All the medical experts agreed that Mr. Weber's aortic dissection had not been survivable, based on the extent of damage seen on the CT scan images.

There was no way the Webers' attorneys had not had the same medical opinion. It was the most consensuses Matt had ever had on a medical opinion, with all five of the firm's retained experts plus an additional two independent consultants reaching the same conclusion.

So what was fueling this lawsuit? Was it Kate's conversation with Mrs. Weber after her husband's death?

Was it greed? He didn't think so. He had learned a lot about Mrs. Weber in his preparation and she didn't seem like the type of woman who would sue for the purpose of undeserved financial gain. Was it love? The couple, by all reported accounts, had been devoted to each other, but, that being said, being in love and losing that loved one alone didn't typically lead to multimillion-dollar lawsuits. That left guilt. Guilt could lead to just about any action, as he could attest to, based on his own past actions.

The question he had to answer now was what was there for Mrs. Weber to feel guilt about to the point she would want Mr. Weber's death legally proclaimed the fault of Boston General and the medical staff responsible for his care?

Typically, this was the point in the case where the firm's private investigators would take over and within one to two months would produce the report he needed. But he didn't have that kind of time.

He read the file again and then picked up the phone. "Hello," the voice of a woman answered on the other end.

"Mrs. Weber, this is Matt McKayne. I represent Boston General in the lawsuit that has been brought against them. I was wondering if we could meet? You are welcome to bring your attorney along, of course, if that would make you feel more comfortable." Matt waited as there was no response other than the sound of her breathing.

"Why should I meet with you, Mr. McKayne?" she asked tentatively.

"Because I want to do the right thing, Mrs. Weber. For your sake, as much as that of everyone else involved in this case." He was being sincere. Mrs. Weber

would eventually lose this case and the longer it went
on the more legal expenses she would have, with nothing gained except for more unresolved grief.

"I need to discuss it with my attorney."

"Of course. Ask him to contact my office and we can
meet whenever you are ready. I appreciate you talking
to me today." He had no anger towards this woman, despite that fact that she was responsible for the lawsuit
that could destroy everything Kate had worked for. If
the lawsuit was successful, everything he had given up
would have been for nothing. But Mrs. Weber was also
a widow. She had already lost her husband, the love of
her life. She had lost enough. Matt couldn't be angry
with her, however misguided her actions had become.

"We'll be in touch, Mr. McKayne. Goodbye."

Forty-five minutes later, her attorney called and an
appointment was made for the day after next. That gave
him forty-eight hours to find the real reason behind the
lawsuit and get the case dropped.

He was missing something. There were facts somewhere that didn't add up, with the case and with Kate
herself. For the first time in his career he felt inferior
to the task at hand. His feelings and involvement with
Kate had led him to change his approach, and his focus
had been on her and not on the facts of the case. Not
that he was succeeding with Kate. Physically, they con-
nected. Emotionally he still felt like they were living
two parallel stories.

He picked up the desk phone again and dialed his
assigned paralegal. "Andy, it's Matt. I want every piece
of information we have on the Boston General case. I
also want the security video from the emergency department waiting room and the triage area for the night
in question."

He didn't wait for a response and hung up immediately. He needed to focus on the case and find the small thread that would lead him to the answer. Would getting the lawsuit dropped win back her trust? He didn't think so. She wanted something more from him and he didn't know what that was. He had already confessed to her the truth about his lie and why he had done it, but that hadn't been enough for her.

Damn, he couldn't think about the case without thinking about Kate and last night. He pulled at the tie around his neck and ran his fingers through his hair, squeezing the tense muscles at the back of his neck. Even with her preoccupation with Chloe's illness, it was going to be impossible to stay away from her. Every part of him wanted to be with her again. It wasn't just the physical desire. It was her letting him hold her that morning in the intensive care unit lounge and for the first time relaxing and not pulling away. It had been a small return to the way they had once been. He passed his hand over his face and straightened his posture. He needed to separate himself physically from her if he had any hope of finding out the truth.

Kate shifted uncomfortably in the bedside chair. It was nine in the evening and the toll of the stress and lack of sleep was building by the hour. She felt new compassion for the family members who "slept" in the chairs every night to be close to their loved ones. Her neck and back ached from the awkward positioning and her heart ached from last night.

So much for closure, she thought to herself. Making love with Matt had done anything but provide closure. It had brought her back to the way they had once been, the way she had once felt, and afterwards she'd had no doubts that she didn't just love him, she was in love with him. Again. Still.

The monitor rang and a white tape was ejected from the machine. She looked at Chloe and her guilt was enormous. It seemed so wrong to be thinking about Matt when Chloe was lying in the intensive care unit intubated and unconscious while her body slowly recovered from the massive insult it had been dealt.

Her red hair made a sharp contrast to the pale hospital linen and the sterility of the room. Hours earlier Kate had brushed it and braided it to the side, trying to maintain some of her friend's dignity in such exposing circumstances. Her face, on the other hand, blended in perfectly, her pallor severe despite all the blood she had received. Kate reached out and curled her fingers around Chloe's. She was surprised at the small twinge she felt in response to the action, a reflex she hadn't expected yet but was grateful for.

"Chloe, it's Kate," she said, though even if Chloe had been conscious she would be physically unable to answer her with the breathing tube in place.

"Chloe, I'm so sorry I let this happen to you. I should have been a better friend to you when you told me you weren't feeling well, instead of focusing on myself and my problems. I promise I'll make it up to you."

She understood family members more at that time than she ever had in her career. The ones who asked the same questions over and over again, so much so that she was late every morning on rounds, the ones who pushed and demanded for more testing and intervention than was being recommended, and the ones who never left the building, despite your assurances and recommendations to do so. She understood perfectly now that they did those things out of love, guilt, and fear; all in a desperate attempt to bring that person back to them the way they had once been.

The alarm rang out again and Kate's focus shifted back to the monitor. Chloe's heart and respiratory rates were elevated beyond the machine's set parameters. She was breathing on her own above the ventilator. She looked back and saw Chloe start to move subtly, her head moving back and forth and her arms and hands testing their strength. The alarm had also triggered her one-on-one nurse to come into the room.

"She's waking up and starting to fight the tube," the nurse assessed quickly.

"Page the doctor on call and ask him to come and see if she can be safely extubated," Kate ordered, temporarily forgetting her role as a friend and not as the physician giving orders.

She reached out and stroked Chloe's hair away from her forehead. "Chloe, it's Kate. Try to stay calm. You are okay. You are intubated and in the intensive care unit but, I promise you, you are okay. You just need to hold on for a few more minutes and I'm going to see if they will take the tube out. If you start panicking they are just going to give you more drugs and leave it in, so you need to stay calm with me for the next few minutes, okay?"

Kate hadn't been sure how conscious Chloe was until her eyes slowly opened and they looked remarkably clear, like she had understood every word Kate had spoken. Kate reached out and squeezed her hand, in part as reassurance and in part to prevent Chloe from instinctively reaching for the tube.

She didn't break eye contact with her for what seemed like hours, but was actually only minutes, before the on-call intensivist arrived.

"Dr. Spence, I'm going to ask you to step out while we go through our extubation check list to make sure it is safe to do so."

She still didn't turn to look at the voice, not wanting to break her connection with Chloe. "Chloe, you heard that. I have to leave for a few minutes while they evaluate you. No room for big dumb surgeons on these occasions. I'm not going to be far away, though, and I'll be back here as soon as they let me, okay?"

She waited for a sign of understanding and felt relieved as Chloe slowly moved her head up and down on the pillow. She squeezed her hand one last time and then let go, leaving the room quickly before she changed her mind and tried to force them to let her stay.

Back in the family waiting room she dug into her bag for her cell phone. She needed to call Tate and tell him about the change in Chloe's condition.

"Tate Reed," he answered instantly, as though his phone had never left his hand.

"It's me. I was just with Chloe and she has regained consciousness and is looking appropriate to extubate. They kicked me out, but the ICU doctor is with her now, so I'm hopeful that they'll take the tube out and she'll be well enough to leave the ICU."

"Is she in pain?" he asked, and Kate was impressed that he seemed to have more surgical sense than she did. She had almost forgotten about the six-inch incision that spanned Chloe's abdomen and which had remained well covered beneath the bed's sheets.

"No, Tate, she didn't seem to be in any pain. She actually seemed just like Chloe, surprisingly beautiful and understanding, even intubated with all the other tubes and wires all around."

"When do you think we can see her?"

"I think these things take about an hour by the time they assemble all the equipment and appropriate staff in case she doesn't do well. But I really don't think she is going to run into a problem."

"I have to start another case in the operating room and it's too late to find someone to cover for me. Can you let me know how she is as soon as you see her again?" Tate was a meticulous and in-control surgeon. He had to be. As a vascular surgeon, his target was everything from the largest to the smallest of blood vessels, with many of his cases being the difference between life and death.

"Of course, but, Tate, I'm really sure she is going to be okay. It's Chloe. I mean, who else goes directly from work to the intensive care unit? I wouldn't be surprised if she tried to take a shift tomorrow," she tried to joke.

"That's not going to happen." Her attempt to lighten the conversation hadn't worked.

"I know, Tate. Go and do your case. I'll call you as soon as I know anything."

"Thanks, Kate."

She glanced again at the phone in her hand, thinking of Matt. A sense of déjà vu passed over her and it was not a welcome one. No messages and no missed calls. Nothing to reassure her she had not just made the same mistake twice.

"Kate." Her thoughts were broken by the sound of her name. Erin Madden was standing in front of her. She glanced at her watch and was surprised to find that an hour had passed and it was almost eleven o'clock. Her fellow resident was dressed as though she had just come from home, in jeans and a casual long-sleeved shirt.

"The intensivist paged me to let me know that Chloe had regained consciousness and had been safely extubated. I need to do her assessment and talk to her and then you can see her."

She had never respected gynecology as much as she had learned to in the past twenty-four hours. It wasn't the roses-and-sunshine specialty the other surgeons thought it was. They really did save lives, this time her best friend's life, and she would be forever grateful. "Okay. Thank you, Erin, for everything."

"It's our job. Kate, I'm probably going to be at least a half an hour if not more. Why don't you get something to eat or take a nap in one of the call rooms? I'll page you when I'm done."

Kate nodded, appreciative of Erin's concern for her well-being and also for the time she was spending on Chloe's care. She watched the petite blonde walk away and decided to take her up on her advice. She walked from the intensive care family lounge to the operating room and found Tate in the recovery room, writing post-operative orders.

He noticed her instantly and she smiled warmly at him, trying to convey the good news before she reached him. "She's been extubated and is doing well. They paged Gynecology as her attending service and Madden is in with her now. It will be another hour before she can have visitors."

"Thanks, Kate."

"Don't thank me. I should have known something was wrong when I saw her the other day and she complained about feeling unwell. Instead, I was too distracted by Matt to notice what was going on with my best friend."

"Kate, you are one of the most important people in Chloe's world. She knows how much you love her and how important she is to you, just as you are to her. You two are inseparable. So stop feeling guilty about a situation you had no involvement in or control over. You know that she would hate that, even more than I do."

"You're right. You know us both really well."

"Yeah…" He paused. "I need to get these orders done and the operative note dictated. I'll go and see Chloe in a few hours after you two have had some time together."

"Thanks, Tate. I'll see you later."

She hurried downstairs towards the hospital coffee shop, happy to have made it before its midnight closing. Too many nights confined to the hospital's vending machines had made their contents completely unappetizing. After getting a cup of tea and a sandwich prepared earlier in the day by the hospital's ladies auxiliary, she made her way back to the intensive care lounge, knowing that she would be more disoriented after thirty minutes of sleep than she would be after none.

She ate the sandwich quickly, having failed to notice how hungry she was until she actually had food in her stomach. She sipped the cup of tea slowly. It was almost a full hour before Erin Madden emerged.

"At least you went for something to eat," she said, smiling and gesturing at the wrapping. "Chloe's doing well. They are going to move her to the obstetric ward in the morning."

"The obstetric ward?" Kate repeated, her confusion clear in her tone.

"Chloe and I both agreed that that would offer her more privacy than any of the other surgical wards, where she might have known or interacted with some of the patients," Erin answered, unfazed by being questioned about her medical decision-making.

"Do you think the nurses there are experienced enough to handle her postoperative care?" Kate asked, still feeling wary of the choice of ward. She had rarely been to the obstetric ward and felt anxious about Chloe being somewhere she didn't know.

"Kate, if there is one thing Obstetrics is good at, it is management of bleeding."

"Okay," Kate agreed. She couldn't dispute the quality of care Chloe had already received and had to trust the team taking care of her. Particularly as she still didn't know what exactly had happened to Chloe.

"I'm sure I'll see you tomorrow. Try not to totally exhaust yourself, Kate. I promise you, if anything changes you'll know as soon as I do."

"Thanks, Erin. Have a good night."

She walked back to Chloe's room and found her asleep in her bed. She no longer had the breathing tube and without the sound of the ventilator, the room was much quieter. Chloe opened her eyes as Kate moved back towards the bedside chair.

"Hey," Chloe croaked, her throat still raw from the irritation of the tube.

"Hey, yourself," Kate replied, unable to keep herself from smiling at the joy of just being able to have this conversation.

"I'm sorry I scared you," Chloe whispered.

Kate reached out and took her hand, fighting for control of her emotions as she said the words that had been repeating in her head since the call. "I'm sorry that I wasn't there for you."

"Kate, there was nothing you could have done."

"Do you want to tell me what happened?" Kate asked gently.

"Not tonight. It's too complicated and I'm too tired and sore to understand the situation myself. Is that okay?"

It was a complete role reversal. Chloe was asking for understanding without explanation, the same thing Kate had wanted when they had first met.

"Of course it's okay, Chloe. Anything you want."

"Anything I want?" she replied. A little flicker of her usual self in her eyes, as one eyebrow arched upwards.

"Anything you want," Kate reaffirmed. She was ready and willing to agree to anything for Chloe.

"Go home, Kate, you look almost as bad as I must." She laughed and then had to brace her stomach because the movement caused her pain. Then laughed again at her action.

"Nice, Chloe." Kate laughed quietly. "Are you sure? I don't mind staying."

"I know. And you also know that all I'm going to do tonight is sleep, so you should go home and do the same."

"I hate it that you are so selfless and reasonable, but I'll do as I'm told. Tate is working nights this week. He's going to stop by in a couple of hours to check in."

"Thanks for the warning."

"Behave yourself while I'm gone. Can't have you cheating on me with any other surgeons, now, can I?"

Chloe laughed again, clutching her stomach. "Get out of here before I need more pain medication just for the laughter."

"'Night, Chloe. I love you."

"'Night, Kate. I know you love me and I love you too."

Kate got home shortly after midnight, exhaustion seeping through her the moment she opened her apartment door. Her eyes immediately fell on her black sweater and

bra, which were still strewn on the living-room floor.
The ones she had pulled off herself the night before.

The bed wasn't made. The sheets were tangled and
she could still see Matt lying there, the memory strong
in her mind. She changed quickly into her pajamas and
walked out of the room back to her couch. She curled
up on its familiar comfort, shut her eyes, trying to block
out the events of the past thirty-six hours, and begged
for sleep.

It didn't come and she lay exhausted, her mind refusing to quiet or slow down and think rationally. She
oscillated between anxieties at not being with Chloe, to
pain from not hearing from Matt. Why hadn't he called?

She officially gave up hope at around four in the
morning and went back to the hospital. Quietly she re-
took her place at Chloe's bedside, assuaging at least
once source of torment. At exactly eight in the morning she couldn't take the waiting any more and called
Matt's firm. The main receptionist put her through to
Matt's office.

"Hello, Matt McKayne's office, this is Andy." Disappointment ricocheted through her as she realized it
was not Matt himself answering.

"It's Dr. Kate Spence, I'm looking for Mr. McKayne."

"Mr. McKayne has returned to New York. Can I
pass on a message?"

She felt her breath leave her but was incapable of taking in more air. This wasn't happening, this couldn't
be happening, could it? Would Matt really leave? Now?
After everything? After they had made love? Her mind
and her heart both knew the answers to her questions.

"No message, thank you."

CHAPTER TWELVE

MATT SAT IN his New York penthouse, the normally minimalist look of his home now overwhelmed with papers strewn across every surface. He didn't usually work from home, but with only a few days to find the missing piece of the puzzle he didn't want to risk any interruptions or distractions from other cases.

He had started with the medical reports and the reviews by the medical experts. Nothing appeared amiss. Mr. Weber had had a Stanford A aortic dissection. It had involved the major branches of the aorta and was a lethal state; there had been no hope of saving him and unfortunately no warning signs of the condition prior to him presenting to hospital that would have alerted him or his family to the impending crisis. The delay in reaching Dr. Reed had been unfortunate, but in no way had it led to the man's death. The attempt at surgical intervention had been an exercise in futility from the beginning.

The firm's legal assistants had taken depositions from every health care worker involved in Mr. Weber's care that night. The plaintiff's counsel had done the same. Matt's junior colleagues were charged with reading and summarizing them, highlighting any points in their favor or causes for concern. He had complete faith in the people who worked for him. He had selected each team member himself and had overseen enough of the cases they had worked on to know he could trust the quality of their work. But this case was different. Something wasn't adding up and it wouldn't stop nagging at him until he could reassure himself that he had looked over every fact and piece of information personally.

He glanced at the clock that was perched on the fireplace mantel. It was two in the morning. He had to leave to go back to Boston the following day and felt like he was running out of time. He flexed his back and shoulders, trying to ease the tension that was building knots in the muscles. Kate hadn't called. He hadn't expected her to, between Chloe and her job, but it still bothered him that she hadn't. He wondered what she had said in her messages all those years ago.

He rose from the kitchen table that he had never used for eating and walked into his state-of-the-art granite and stainless-steel kitchen, also rarely used for its intended purpose. His only appliance on its smooth stone counters was an espresso machine that he had never been as grateful for as he was tonight. As he waited for the machine to produce the espresso shots to top with brewed coffee, he fixated on Kate. What was she doing right now?

He tried again to block her from his mind and resisted the temptation to call her. It was late and if there was the small possibility she was sleeping he did not want to be the cause of disturbing that precious sleep. Instead he took his coffee and the pile of depositions to the comfort of his leather couch. It was the only piece of furniture he had never changed no matter where he lived, much to his designer's dismay. It reminded him of where he had been and his mind and body relaxed as he sank into the cushions and began to read.

Three hours later he was only halfway through the pile and he was getting sloppy. The last deposition had taken him twice as long to get through as it should have and he finally surrendered to the need for sleep. He rose from the couch and went to his bedroom, climbing into the king-size bed. Time was running out for him and for Kate.

He was awoken from sleep later in the morning by the sound of his cell phone. It took him a few seconds before he remembered where he was and was able to answer the call.

"McKayne."

"Are you really gone?" Kate's voice wavered over the phone and he didn't miss the hurt or the accusation in her voice.

"Kate."

"It's an easy question, Matt."

"Yes, I'm back in New York."

"I'm a fool."

"No, Kate, you don't understand. I'm trying to help you."

"That's what you said about last time, Matt. It didn't make it okay then and it doesn't make it okay now."

"Kate, when are you going to trust me again?" He was tired of this; he had been honest with her and there was nothing else he could do. He waited as time passed in silence.

"How can you ask me to trust you after everything?"

"I thought we had gotten past that."

"No, Matt. Another night together hasn't fixed our past. I still remember you leaving. I still remember being discarded and replaced."

"Replaced?"

"Your sexual exploits were very popular in the New York society pages your first year in New York, Matt."

He cringed. He wasn't proud of his behavior that year, but he wasn't going to defend it now, not so many years later and definitely not over the phone, when Kate was clearly trying to use it as an excuse to drive a wedge between them.

"Where is this coming from, Kate?" He waited again for her answer, all of his senses alert now and focused on her.

"I can't believe you left. I feel so stupid for everything. I won't let you hurt me, Matt, not again. You may not be able to say it, but I can. Goodbye."

The click was unmistakable. He phoned her back and the call went straight to voicemail. He didn't try again: her message had been loud and clear.

He showered but skipped shaving, not wanting to waste any of the time he had left. He returned to the stack of files and worked steadily for the next ten hours, his focus unwavering. Nothing was out of place or suspect. The overwhelming sentiment in all of the depositions was of support for Drs. Reed and Spence. All their actions were deemed not only professional as per the standard of care but also excellent in their quality. Those who had worked with the two together that night had seen nothing in their interaction that had even hinted at a change in the personal nature of their relationship.

His stomach growled and he realized that he had neglected to eat any of the delivered food from earlier. He went to the brown bags and brought them into the living room, where he prepared to watch, while he ate, the emergency department surveillance tapes his assistant had retrieved. He inserted the first disk into the DVD player and noted the time on the bottom of the screen. It was five-twenty in the afternoon, several hours before Mr. Weber had presented. He reached over to grab the remote to fast-forward the tape to later in the evening when something caught his eye.

He watched as Mr. and Mrs. Weber entered the emergency department and checked in at the triage desk. They spoke with the triage nurse and then after several minutes left the department and the hospital itself through the main doors. Matt was stunned. Nowhere in any of the medical charts was this interaction described. He didn't move from his spot for the next several hours, watching every second of footage in real time, afraid that something else might be hidden in the tapes.

Mr. Weber and his wife arrived back in the emergency department at nine twenty-three that evening by ambulance. The ambulance bay bypassed the main triage desk so the nurse who talked with them earlier would have had no knowledge of their reappearance in the department. From that point on every moment of his hospital care had been documented and was recorded accurately in the case files.

Matt picked up the phone and called Jeff Sutherland's cell phone, disregarding the time of day. "Jeff, it's Matt McKayne. Does the hospital track patients who present to the emergency department and then leave without being assessed by a physician?"

"Yes. Those charts are kept in a separate area, to be used for future needs assessment and capacity planning."

"But do they have the patient's identifying information on them?" Matt asked, wanting more than just the video to back his argument.

"Yes. They also have the presenting complaint as

listed by the triage nurse and any other information collected during the encounter."

"Good. I'm flying back to Boston tomorrow morning and will meet you at eight. I need you to take me to where the files are stored so we can get access to a file. I also need you find the nurse who was working the emergency department triage desk the late afternoon to early evening of Mr. Weber's death. I want to speak with her tomorrow at eight-thirty."

"Are you going to tell me what's going on, Mr. McKayne?" Sutherland asked, obviously not used to being on the side of accepting orders.

"Not yet, but if things work out, by this time tomorrow I should be able to tell you everything."

"Okay. I'll see you in the morning. Good night."

Matt stood in the large conference room, staring out the windows, waiting for Mrs. Weber and her attorney to arrive. He hadn't felt this level of pride in his work for years. He hadn't tried to call Kate again, knowing that he needed to bring something different to their circular conversations of the past.

His eagerness faded when Mrs. Weber entered the conference room with her attorney. She was the same age as his mother. Her once blonde hair was peppered with gray and she had a kindness to her face that shamed Matt. The problem with winning a case was that it meant someone else had to lose and today that would be Mrs. Weber. He smiled politely and genuinely at her, taking no joy in what he was about to do.

"Thank you both for coming today. Please, take a seat. Can we get you anything, tea, coffee, water?"

"A glass of water would be nice," she answered, looking nervously around the room.

He gestured to his assistant and took a seat on the opposite side of the table, trying to do everything in his power to make Mrs. Weber feel comfortable for the conversation they were about to have. He had purposefully kept the number of people from his firm down to only him and his assistant, guessing it was probably going to be a painful discussion for her.

"What did you want to discuss, Mr. McKayne?" her attorney asked confidently. Matt glared at the opposing counsel. He was in his mid-forties and had dressed in an overpriced suit that was designed to be recognized for its brand and not the cut and quality of the design. His hair was receding and he had a hungry look in his eyes as he surveyed the scale of the boardroom.

Half of Matt's passion for medical defense stemmed from his hatred of men like Mrs. Weber's attorney. They were vultures who preyed on the misfortune of others for their own gain. There were a few who represented those who were truly victims of malpractice, but the vast majority were opportunists. Mrs. Weber's attorney was a pure opportunist. No malpractice attorney worthy of the title would have taken this case, and Mrs. Weber's money, with all the expert opinions so in favor of the hospital's care. If the man thought Matt wanted to discuss a settlement, he was going to be sorely disappointed.

Matt completely disregarded the other attorney and focused all his attention on Mrs. Weber. "Mrs. Weber, the night your husband died you brought him to the emergency department yourself earlier in the evening." It wasn't a question; it was a statement, delivered as gently as he could in the circumstances.

Her eyes widened and Matt knew in an instant that

everything he'd uncovered was indeed correct. He didn't wait for her to answer.

"I had our medical experts reexamine your husband's death. Even if you had convinced him to stay that night when you first came in, he would still have died from the aortic dissection."

"I tried to get him to stay, but when the triage nurse said it was up to a six-hour wait, Michael refused. I thought because the nurse had checked his blood pressure and pulse that he wasn't that sick." It was the panicked explanation of a woman who still didn't understand what had gone wrong.

"Stop talking, Marion," her attorney instructed her harshly. Matt turned and glared at the creep and within seconds he shrank back into his chair. Matt directed his attention back to Mrs. Weber, who was crying and trying to wipe away the evidence with the sleeve of her cardigan.

"I know," he started gently. "The triage nurse remembered you from that night because of how strongly you tried to talk him into staying. You did your best, Marion. There was nothing the triage nurse, you or Michael could have known or done that night to prevent what happened. Just as there is nothing that Drs. Spence and Reed could have done, but they tried—just as you did."

The woman crumpled before him and Matt could feel no joy at discovering the truth. He passed her the box of tissues he had left on the conference-room table and waited for her, not wanting to diminish her grief by interrupting.

"I just needed it not to be my fault. I wasn't interested in the money. I just wanted the court to say 'Yes, it was the doctors' fault' so that I would know for sure it wasn't mine. I miss him so much."

"It wasn't your fault, Marion," he said, as clearly and firmly as he could. She looked at him and he maintained eye contact. "It wasn't your fault."

The sympathetic tone in his voice faded when he shifted his attention to Mrs. Weber's attorney. "I expect you to file the papers to drop the case before the end of the week. I also expect your firm to cover the entire cost of this case. It should never have gotten this far and you and your firm are going to take the blame and shoulder whatever costs have been incurred. I'll be keeping in touch with Mrs. Weber and if I hear that she has received any type of invoice or attempt to request payment from you I will personally represent her *pro bono* in actions against you for negligence and misrepresentation. Do I make myself clear?"

"Perfectly," the man remarked snidely. Although it annoyed him, Matt let it go as he was certain the lawyer had gotten the message.

"You can leave now. I'll make sure Mrs. Weber gets home." The man rose from the table and left the room without even addressing Marion Weber. Matt motioned for his assistant to leave and he walked around the table to sit at Mrs. Weber's side.

"I'm so sorry for my actions, Mr. McKayne. Can you please let Dr. Spence and Dr. Reed know that? I was so lost without him, I couldn't tell right from wrong. I think even if the lawsuit had been successful I still would have always wondered if I had really been responsible. At least I know now there was nothing I could have done. Maybe I can start to move past that night and focus on the forty-two wonderful years that came before it."

"That sounds like an excellent plan, Mrs. Weber. I'll definitely pass that along to Drs. Reed and Spence. They know how much you loved your husband and have no hard feelings towards you. Can I arrange for our driver to take you home?" He rose from the table and helped her to her feet, wanting to make sure she was steady before he let go.

"Yes, that would be very nice. Thank you, Mr. Mc-Kayne, for everything today." Matt was startled when she put her arms up and hugged him, but he instinctively hugged her back, her blonde head barely reaching his chest.

"Let's get you home," he said, gently waiting for her to let go before letting go himself and walking her back to his assistant to make the necessary arrangements. Once he was sure she was safely taken care of, he went back to the conference room to pick up his files. He paused and glanced out over the Boston skyline. He had been the type of man he wanted to be today. Kate had done that.

CHAPTER THIRTEEN

SHE STILL WASN'T answering her phone. Matt walked through the lobby of Boston General, searching for Kate. He didn't want to page her in case she was operating, but he also wanted to see and talk to her as soon as possible. The past days without her had seemed almost as long as the nine years they had been apart. He had discovered the motivation behind Mrs. Weber's actions and now he was determined to do the same with Kate.

If she wasn't with a patient, she would be with Chloe, he thought to himself. He went to the admitting office and turned on the charm to get Chloe's room information. He was surprised to be directed towards the obstetrics ward and verified the information twice, before departing for the fourth-floor unit. The pink and blue pastel walls of the unit were different from anywhere else he had seen in the hospital. He made his way towards the front desk and the unit clerk seated at it.

"I'm looking for room 4501."

"Dr. Darcy is not having any visitors," the clerk replied, not needing to reference the room number with the patient bed list. This was obviously not the first time she had delivered this news.

"Can you please ask her if she would be willing to see Matt McKayne?" He smiled warmly and smoothly at the clerk, using his charms again, and she seemed to have a change of heart, rounding the desk to go check with Chloe.

'I know Kate better than anyone,' Chloe had said the first and only time they had met. Maybe if he couldn't find Kate, he could start searching for answers with Chloe.

"Dr. Darcy said you can go ahead—last room on the left at the end of the hall."

He walked into the room and was taken aback at the sight of Chloe. The feisty redhead he had met in Tate's office had been replaced by a fragile-looking woman in a hospital bed.

"It's not contagious." She laughed, attuned to his reaction. The action made her grab at her stomach and groan with regret.

She's still there, he thought to himself, and walked into the room, shutting the door and taking the chair by her bed. "How are you feeling?" he asked.

"Like I got hit by a bus, thank you for asking. Why are you really here, Matt?" She was direct and completely disarming.

"I was looking for Kate, or at the least some information about Kate." Chloe would see through anything other than the truth and he had nothing to lose or hide.

"Do you really think that's a good idea?" she asked without scorn. Chloe had obviously gained some knowledge about his and Kate's past together since they'd first met a few weeks ago. He wanted and needed to know what Kate had told her, how Kate was seeing things.

"What do you mean, Chloe?"

With not insignificant effort she pushed herself up on the hospital bed until she was sitting upright and staring him directly in the eye. "I mean that Kate was really messed up when we first met at Columbia and I won't let that happen again."

"Columbia?" Matt felt all the air leave the room and he stared at Chloe, waiting for her to correct her error.

"Yes, Columbia. We both went to medical school at Columbia University in New York City. I believe you are familiar with the institution, given that's where you apparently went to law school?"

Chloe was staring at him, eyebrows arched, waiting for a response. He didn't have one. Kate had gone to Columbia for medical school. She had been there the entire time. When he'd thought he'd heard her voice or seen her on campus, he had. When he'd seen the woman in the coffee shop who had reminded him so much of her that he'd had to leave, it had to have been her. She had found a way for them to be together and he had taken the now seemingly easy route and ruined it. She had been stronger than he had given her credit for. She had also probably been strong enough to survive his family, he just hadn't believed in her the same way she had obviously believed in him.

The other night he had vowed to her that if she had been in New York, nothing would have kept him from her, but she *had* been in New York, at Columbia. He had deserved that slap. He actually deserved much worse and he now completely understood why Kate didn't trust him.

"Matt? Matt?" Chloe's voice broke through his thoughts. "Hello-o-o, are you all right?"

"I didn't know," he responded absently. He had come for answers and he had gotten them. He looked at Chloe and felt grateful for her help amidst his shock. "Thank you, Chloe."

He walked out of the hospital room while a maelstrom of thoughts and emotions charged through his mind. He would never forgive himself for what he had done, so how could he expect Kate to?

Kate walked through the corridors of Boston General with more foreboding than she had the afternoon Matt had walked back into her life. Once again she was being summoned to a meeting with the hospital's senior administrators and this time she didn't waste what little energy she had left worrying about the reason behind the last-minute request.

She reached the corridor outside the main boardroom and saw Tate leaning against the wall, looking equally as unimpressed with the circumstances.

"Do you know what this is about?" he asked, apparently having received no more information than she had.

"No idea," she sighed, coming to a stop beside him.

"Well, I guess there's only one way to find out." He led the way into the room where it had all begun. The conference room was filled with all the same men, except that Matt wasn't there. She immediately felt crushing disappointment. Her heart and mind were still trying to relearn to live without him, while at the same time she felt angry at herself for loving someone so deeply who had proved repeatedly how little he loved her back.

"Take a seat, Drs. Reed and Spence," Jeff invited them both. This time they took chairs side by side, united in whatever was about to occur. "We have some information we would like to share with you."

She held her breath and braced herself for whatever was about to be said. Her personal life was in a shambles and she felt like her career was hanging by a precarious thread.

"Tate, Kate," Dr. Williamson started. "I am pleased

to inform you that the Weber family has dropped the lawsuit against Boston General and yourselves. They have also agreed to sign an agreement against any future legal action."

Kate felt her jaw drop and quickly looked at Tate for confirmation. He looked equally as surprised and she knew then she had not been wrong in what she had just heard.

"Why the change of heart?" Tate asked the group.

Sutherland answered, "Mr. McKayne discovered some information that helped him understand Mrs. Weber's motivation behind the lawsuit. He met with her this afternoon and after discussing the events of the evening and the medical expert reviews, she no longer felt there was any negligence involved."

Matt had done this. Pride and pain filled her at the same time. He had saved her from what would have been a permanent mark on her career and he hadn't even bothered to tell her himself. Maybe this was his goodbye?

"Thank you all. We appreciate your support throughout this matter," Tate said to the group. She should probably say something similar but no words came to mind and she sat there mutely.

"We value both of you and the work you do for this hospital. We strongly hope, Kate, that you'll consider returning to a staff position once you have completed your fellowship." Dr. Williamson's attention was directly focused on her.

A staff position at Boston General was the job she had wanted for the past five years but in the past six months she had forced herself to give up dreaming about it. After her breakup with Tate she had ruled it out as a possibility. She had been crushed, knowing she was going to have to leave Boston General, the city itself, and especially Chloe, who had accepted a staff position in the emergency department.

"There is nothing I would like more," she answered, but in her heart she knew there was something she wanted much, much more.

"Then consider it a done deal. Now, if you'll excuse us, I think we all have work to do." Dr. Williamson rose and the other men followed suit, leaving the conference room. Kate stood from her chair, her mind still reeling from the events.

"Congratulations, Kate." Tate was smiling at her, but she was still trying to process the developments of the past ten minutes.

"Thanks," she mumbled in return. The lawsuit was over and she had received the job offer she had desperately been working towards, but it wasn't enough. With Matt she remembered what it was like to be happy, even for one night, and nothing felt as it should without him.

When she looked back at Tate his expression had changed. He seemed to be analyzing her with almost as much scrutiny as she had been assessing herself internally. "I take it you're no closer to figuring things out with Matt than the last time we talked?"

"He's gone." She replied with the only fact she was sure of.

"I don't think so, Kate. It sounds like he's still around, judging from our meeting today." Whose side was Tate on? She felt resentment towards both men. She was tired of all the presumptions being made on her behalf. She was going to spend the rest of her life loving a man she couldn't trust and never finding that sense of happiness again.

"I'm too hurt to feel gratitude towards him right now, Tate, so don't ask me to."

"I wouldn't dream of it. What I am going to ask you to do is to go home. You have barely slept or been outside this building since Chloe got sick."

"Is this your way of telling me I look like hell?" Kate replied, a small smile at the corner of her lips.

"No. But I think if you tried to stay with Chloe again tonight, you would worry her more than you would help her."

It was odd, this new relationship with Tate. In almost every way it was new, except that it felt old and comfortable. It was true friendship and instead of their past intimacy making things awkward, it allowed for more honesty between them.

"You're right. She said the same thing last night. I give in. I'm lucky to have you both in my life, and in case you didn't realize it, you are both officially stuck with me."

She walked along the cement sidewalks towards home. The sun was out and the birch trees that lined the street were starting to show signs of spring. She smiled, feeling some peace at knowing this was not going to be her last spring in Boston, just one of many to come. It was going to be hard to go back to New York for her fellowship, but it was going to be worth it. Devoting her career to helping women with breast cancer would at least lay one of her demons to rest.

She had no idea where Matt was going to be or even where he was now. Was he going to stay in Boston, go back to New York, or was there somewhere else in the world where he spent his time? It was going to haunt her, not knowing where he was. She didn't want to have to worry about any more accidental encounters that would cause a resurfacing of feelings she wanted to move past. Still, she refused to call him, not again. She had finally said her goodbye.

She was lost in thought as she approached her apartment building. She looked up just as she reached the base of the stairs and stopped dead. Matt was sitting on her steps. He was still dressed in a business suit and hunched over with his forearms resting on his legs, hands clasped together. He looked as disconcerted as she felt surprised to see him again.

She decided not to make the experience any more painful than it needed to be and instead of challenging him took the spot next to him on the concrete, avoiding looking at him as she stared vaguely in the same direction he was looking across the street. In contrast to the cool concrete against her bottom she felt Matt's natural warmth radiating from him along her side. It reminded her of making love with him and it took every ounce of willpower not to cry at the memory.

"I don't deserve you." Matt's painfully confessed words broke into her internal battle.

Of all the things she had expected to hear, that was not it. Matt had always felt right in all his actions. Even when he'd confessed to lying to her about not loving her, he still had tried to justify his actions as being for her own good. When he had told Tate about them, it had been the right and honorable thing to do. After spending a decade not feeling like she was enough for Matt, it was surreal to hear him confess that he was the one who wasn't good enough for her. She couldn't respond, didn't know how to respond.

"I didn't know you were in New York. I wanted so badly to be with you that I erased all your messages and emails before I listened to or read them so as to do everything in my power to keep myself away from you. I thought I was doing the right thing for you." He sounded so honest, but she didn't believe what he was saying.

"Matt, you saw me in the coffee shop that spring. You took one look at me, turned your back and walked away from me. No looking back, no second glance." No more lies, no more misunderstandings, she was going to let everything out this time. It was the only way she was ever going to heal.

He reached out and took her hand, her small one completely engulfed in his. She didn't say anything and still couldn't bring herself to look him in the eye, so instead she concentrated on the sight of their hands together.

"I honestly thought I was hallucinating. I had already thought I had imagined your voice, and seen you on campus, so when I walked into the coffee shop and saw you that day, I thought it was my mind imagining what I so desperately wanted to see."

Her mind whirled with his last confession. She tried to put together the facts of the past, with her perceptions and now Matt's. She started talking and wasn't sure for whose benefit she was speaking.

"I need to understand this, Matt, because I can't tell what's true anymore. You're saying you were in love with me the night we first made love and you lied because you thought it was the right thing for me? You're also saying that you didn't know that I was in New York with you, and that you wanted to be with me so badly that you thought you imagined me the day you walked away from me in the coffee shop? And now you're saying that you know all this and you don't deserve me?"

"I'm saying that I loved you then and I still love you, but I know now I don't deserve you."

She let go of his hand abruptly and their eyes met for the first time in the conversation.

"When do I get to decide what I deserve, Matt? When do I get to decide what's best for me? Because I decided nine years ago that you were worth changing my life for and it's about time you let me make my own decisions because I love you, still, and always will."

As her last words echoed around them, Matt reached over and pulled Kate towards him. He held her close as his arms drew around her and his lips found hers. For the first time in their relationship there was nothing left unsaid. There were no thoughts about what the kiss meant or what the ramifications would be; instead, there was just love and honesty between them.

When they finally broke apart, he kissed her forehead and rested his against hers. Kate smiled. "Marry me?" he asked quietly. "I never want to be away from you ever again."

Kate's smile widened and she worked her hands between his shirt and jacket, feeling his shoulder blades beneath her fingers and holding him closer to her. It wasn't just happiness she felt, it was a sense of contentment and peace.

"Yes, I'll marry you, Matt. And you never have to be away from me again. You just have to agree to move to New York for two years and then back to Boston permanently because I've accepted a position at Boston General after my fellowship, and this time it's your turn to move."

He lifted away from her and smiled the same Matt grin she had fallen in love with so many years ago. "Anything for you, Katie. Always."

* * * * *

Work hard, play harder...

Welcome to the Gold Coast, where hearts are broken as quickly as they are healed. Featuring some of the rising stars of the medical world, this new four-book series dives headfirst into Surfer's Paradise.

Available as a bundle at
www.millsandboon.co.uk/medical

Join the Mills & Boon Book Club

Want to read more **Medical** books?
We're offering you **2 more** absolutely **FREE!**

We'll also treat you to these fabulous extras:

- Exclusive offers and much more!
- FREE home delivery
- FREE books and gifts with our special rewards scheme

Get your free books now!

visit **www.millsandboon.co.uk/bookclub**
or call Customer Relations on **020 8288 2888**

The World of Mills & Boon®

There's a Mills & Boon® series that's perfect for you. We publish ten series and, with new titles every month, you never have to wait long for your favourite to come along.

By Request

Relive the romance with the best of the best
12 stories every month

Cherish

Experience the ultimate rush of falling in love
12 new stories every month

Desire

Passionate and dramatic love stories
6 new stories every month

n o c t u r n e

An exhilarating underworld of dark desires
Up to 3 new stories every mon